Terrifying Tales to Tell at Night

Terrifying Tales to Tell at Night

10 SCARY STORIES TO GIVE YOU NIGHTMARES!

Selected by Stephen Jones

with drawings by RANDY BROECKER

Sky Pony Press
New York

Sky Pony Press books may be purchased in bulk at special discounts for sales promotion, corporate gifts, fund-raising, or educational purposes. Special editions can also be created to specifications. For details, contact the Special Sales Department, Sky Pony Press, 307 West 36th Street, 11th Floor, New York, NY 10018 or info@skyhorsepublishing.com.

Sky Pony® is a registered trademark of Skyhorse Publishing, Inc.®, a Delaware corporation.

Visit our website at www.skyponypress.com.

10 9 8 7 6 5 4 3 2

Library of Congress Cataloging-in-Publication Data is available on file.
Library of Congress Control Number: 2019944850

Cover design by Brian Peterson
Cover illustration credit by Randy Broecker

ISBN: 978-1-5107-5124-8
Ebook ISBN: 978-1-5107-5125-5

Printed in the United States of America

CONTENTS

"Here comes a candle to light you to bed,
And here comes a chopper to chop off your head!"
—Traditional English nursery rhyme

INTRODUCTION

I'M WARNING YOU. The stories in this book are scary. *Real* scary! So I don't want you complaining to me that, after reading them, you couldn't sleep or they upset you. That's your problem. The clue is in the title of the book.

However, if you enjoy being scared, or love ghosts, or monsters, or nasty old grannies, then this is the volume for you! You'll find all these things, and more, in the following pages . . .

You probably know Neil Gaiman as the bestselling author of *Coraline* and *The Graveyard Book*, and in "Click-clack the Rattlebag" he introduces us to the monstrous Click-clacks. who come from the dark to spirit away those who aren't paying attention—and drink their *insides*.

Rodney meets a descendant of Doctor Frankenstein who is trying his hand at a spot of monster-making in R. Chetwynd-Hayes's humorous story "Homemade Monster," while in Lynda E. Rucker's "The Sideways Lady," a group of children go searching for an old legend in a reputedly haunted house on Halloween. What could possibly go wrong?

If you've ever been bullied at school, or embarrassed by a teacher, then you're going to enjoy what happens to Charles in "Here There Be Tygers" by probably the most famous horror author in the world, Stephen King.

Another tremulous young boy is afraid of what will visit him on Christmas Eve down "The Chimney" by Ramsey Campbell, and Bart Setwick discovers something very odd about his three new friends at the "School for the Unspeakable" by veteran pulp magazine writer Manly Wade Wellman.

Our second Christmas story is "Granny's Grinning" by author and playwright Robert Shearman, who brought the Daleks back to TV's *Doctor Who*. It's a nasty tale all about Sarah's elderly grandmother, and the husband she still misses and wants back . . .

Lisa Morton is an expert on Halloween, but her story "The Chemistry of Ghosts" is about a brother and sister who go on a ghost hunt and discover more than they bargained for when they encounter a phantom teacher who sets them a puzzle to be solved.

"The Man Who Drew Cats" was the first story novelist and screenwriter Michael Marshall Smith ever published. He has always been a fan of the work of Ray Bradbury and Stephen King, and you will find the influence of both in this tale of how a boy and his mother are saved from their tormentor one hot summer night.

Finally, in Charles L. Grant's story "Are You Afraid of the Dark?" three boys find themselves playing a terrifying game with a babysitter from Hell.

And then there's Randy Broecker's creepy drawings. If the stories are not enough to send a chill up your spine, then his artwork certainly is. Or else you are made of sterner stuff than I am.

So, there you are—a book of scary stories and illustrations that should keep you entertained for a few hours and hopefully will have you looking over your shoulder every now and again. Why don't you read this book aloud to your friends around a campfire or by flashlight with a brother or sister before bedtime? And, once you've finished reading it, why not have a competition with them to see if the story they found the most terrifying is the same one that you did?

But remember . . . once you've read this book from cover to cover, please do not hold *me* responsible for your—or anybody else's—nightmares!

I warned you.

—Stephen Jones

CLICK-CLACK
THE RATTLEBAG
Neil Gaiman

"BEFORE YOU TAKE me up to bed, will you tell me a story?"

"Do you actually need me to take you up to bed?" I asked the boy.

He thought for a moment. Then, with intense seriousness, "Yes, actually I think you do. It's because of, I've finished my homework, and so it's my bedtime, and I am a bit scared. Not very scared. Just a bit. But it is a very big house, and lots of times the lights don't work and it's a sort of dark."

I reached over and tousled his hair.

"I can understand that," I said. "It is a very big old house." He nodded. We were in the kitchen, where it was light and warm. I put down my magazine on the kitchen table. "What kind of story would you like me to tell you?"

"Well," he said, thoughtfully. "I don't think it should be *too* scary, because then when I go up to bed, I will just be thinking about monsters the whole time. But if it isn't just a *little* bit scary then I won't be interested. And you make up scary stories, don't you? I know she says that's what you do."

"She exaggerates. I write stories, yes. Nothing that's been published, yet, though. And I write lots of different kinds of stories."

"But you *do* write scary stories?"

"Yes."

The boy looked up at me from the shadows by the door, where he was waiting. "Do you know any stories about Click-clack the Rattlebag?"

"I don't think so."

"Those are the best sorts of stories."

"Do they tell them at your school?"

He shrugged. "Sometimes."

"What's a Click-clack the Rattlebag story?"

He was a precocious child, and was unimpressed by his sister's boyfriend's ignorance. You could see it on his face. "Everybody knows them."

"I don't," I said, trying not to smile.

He looked at me as if he was trying to decide whether or not I was pulling his leg. He said, "I think maybe you should take me up to my bedroom, and then you can tell me a story before I go to sleep, but a very not-scary story because I'll be up in my bedroom then, and it's actually a bit dark up there, too."

I said, "Shall I leave a note for your sister, telling her where we are?"

"You can. But you'll hear when they get back. The front door is very slammy."

We walked out of the warm and cozy kitchen into the hallway of the big house, where it was chilly and draughty and dark. I flicked the light switch, but nothing happened.

"The bulb's gone," the boy said. "That always happens."

Our eyes adjusted to the shadows. The moon was almost full, and blue-white moonlight shone in through the high windows on the staircase, down into the hall. "We'll be all right," I said.

"Yes," said the boy, soberly. "I am very glad you're here." He seemed less precocious now. His hand found mine, and he held onto my fingers comfortably, trustingly, as if he'd known me all his life. I felt responsible and adult. I did not know if the feeling I had for his sister, who was my girlfriend, was love, not yet, but I liked that the child treated me as one of the family. I felt like his big brother, and I stood taller, and if there was something unsettling about the empty house I would not have admitted it for worlds.

The stairs creaked beneath the threadbare stair-carpet.

"Click-clacks," said the boy, "are the best monsters ever."

"Are they from television?"

"I don't think so. I don't think any people know where they come from. Mostly they come from the dark."

"Good place for a monster to come."

"Yes."

We walked along the upper corridor in the shadows, walking from patch of moonlight to patch of moonlight. It really was a big house. I wished I had a flashlight.

"They come from the dark," said the boy, holding onto my hand. "I think probably they're made of dark. And they come in when you don't pay attention. That's when they come in. And then they take you back to their . . . not nests. What's a word that's like *nests*, but not?"

"House?"

"No. It's not a house."

"Lair?"

He was silent. Then, "I think that's the word, yes. Lair." He squeezed my hand. He stopped talking.

"Right. So they take the people who don't pay attention back to their lair. And what do they do then, your monsters? Do they suck all the blood out of you, like vampires?"

He snorted. "Vampires don't suck all the blood out of you. They only drink a little bit. Just to keep them going, and, you know, flying around. Click-clacks are much scarier than vampires."

"I'm not scared of vampires," I told him.

"Me neither. I'm not scared of vampires either. Do you want to know what Click-clacks do? They drink you," said the boy.

"Like a Coke?"

"Coke is very bad for you," said the boy. "If you put a tooth in Coke, in the morning, it will be dissolved into nothing. That's how bad coke is for you and why you must always clean your teeth, every night."

I'd heard the Coke story as a boy, and had been told, as an adult, that it wasn't true, but was certain that a lie which promoted dental hygiene was a good lie, and I let it pass.

"Click-clacks drink you," said the boy. "First they bite you, and then you go all *ishy* inside, and all your meat and all your brains and everything except your bones and your skin turns into a wet, milkshakey stuff and then the Click-clack sucks it out through the holes where your eyes used to be."

"That's disgusting," I told him. "Did you make it up?"

We'd reached the last flight of stairs, all the way in to the big house.

"No."

"I can't believe you kids make up stuff like that."

"You didn't ask me about the Rattlebag," he said.

"Right. What's the Rattlebag?"

"Well," he said, sagely, soberly, a small voice from the darkness beside me, "once you're just bones and skin, they hang you up on a hook, and you rattle in the wind."

"So what do these Click-clacks look like?" Even as I asked him, I wished I could take the question back, and leave it unasked. I thought: *Huge spidery creatures. Like the one in the shower that morning.* I'm afraid of spiders.

I was relieved when the boy said, "They look like what you aren't expecting. What you aren't paying attention to."

We were climbing wooden steps now. I held on to the railing on my left, held his hand with my right, as he walked beside me. It smelled like dust and old wood, that high in the house. The boy's tread was certain, though, even though the moonlight was scarce.

"Do you know what story you're going to tell me, to put me to bed?" he asked. "It doesn't actually have to be scary."

"Not really."

"Maybe you could tell me about this evening. Tell me what you did?"

"That won't make much of a story for you. My girl-friend just moved in to a new place on the edge of town. She inherited it from an aunt or someone. It's very big and very old. I'm going to spend my first night with her, tonight, so I've been waiting for an hour or so for her and her housemates to come back with the wine and an Indian takeaway."

"See?" said the boy. There was that precocious amuse-ment again. But all kids can be insufferable sometimes, when they think they know something you don't. It's probably good for them. "You know all that. But you don't think. You just let your brain fill in the gaps."

He pushed open the door to the attic room. It was perfectly dark, now, but the opening door disturbed the air, and I heard things rattle gently, like dry bones in thin bags, in the slight wind. Click. Clack. Click. Clack. Like that.

I would have pulled away, then, if I could, but small, firm fingers pulled me forward, unrelentingly, into the dark.

HOMEMADE MONSTER
R. Chetwynd-Hayes

RODNEY WAS LOST.

That should not be possible in twentieth-century England, where there are signposts standing at every crossroads, but Rodney managed to do it. He had been cycling through a network of country lanes and the signposts had not been helpful. They had said CATCHEM WALLOP 1 MILE and UNDER BASHEM 114 MILES, and when he reached these places they proved to be sleepy little villages surrounded by open fields. He could of course have asked someone the way to Benfield, which was his destination, but he was rather shy and found it difficult to approach strangers. So he cycled on, hoping that he would sooner or later reach a main road, and now darkness was falling and it was beginning to rain.

Then his rear tire made a loud popping sound, which was followed by a prolonged sigh, and the bicycle began to wobble across the lane. Rodney dismounted and pushed the machine up a steep incline, wishing he had spent his holiday with his family at Bognor Regis.

The rain simply teemed down, and in no time at all he was drenched. Then there was a vivid flash of lightning and a really ear-splitting clap of thunder, and Rodney, although he tried to be brave, was very frightened indeed. He knew he must not take shelter under a tree, because his father had often said that trees attract lightning, and it was hardly the time to find out if this information was true or not.

He crested the hill, wheeled his bicycle around a sharp bend—and saw the house. It was a very large house, standing well back from the road, and surrounded by an unkempt lawn. No curtains veiled the windows, in fact some were boarded up, and it was reasonable to suppose the place was deserted. So Rodney pushed the rusty iron gate open, parked his machine in the large, crumbling porch, then looked for a way to enter the house.

The front door was locked, but when he made his way around to the back, he found a small window half-open. It only took a few seconds for him to clamber over the sill and take refuge in the room beyond.

Dust covered the floors, damp had loosened the wallpaper and formed brown stains on the ceiling. The place was cold, and, as the window refused to close, Rodney decided to venture farther into the house, hoping that he would find a room with a fireplace so that he could light a fire and dry his clothes.

The door reluctantly, and with many creaking groans, slid open to reveal a gloomy passage. This ended at a large hall where a splendid staircase rose up in a graceful curve to a long gallery. A number of closed doors led away from the hall, and Rodney chose the nearest one, pushed it open, and entered the room beyond. He found himself in what once must have been a luxurious drawing room. The upholstery on the chairs and sofa had rotted, the carpet was hidden under a thick layer of dust, and festoons of cobwebs swayed gently from the high ceiling. But there was a fireplace.

Rodney was wondering what he could use for fuel, when he heard a sudden noise. It was the tramp of heavy feet. A slow, thudding tread that suggested a very large person, who did not believe in hurrying but moved forward with the ponderous approach of a tank.

The footsteps crossed the hall—then stopped, and Rodney realized that his footprints must be clearly imprinted in the dust, leaving a trail to the door of this very room. The footsteps began again and grew louder as they came nearer, then the door trembled, before it flew back and crashed against the wall.

A giant stood in the doorway; a massive figure with a completely bald head and an immense barrel of a chest that was barely covered by a worn leather jerkin. A rumbling sound started way down in the stomach, then rose up and emerged from the creature's throat as booming words.

"What you doing here?"

Rodney gulped and tried to speak without stammering. "I thought the house was empty. It's raining . . ."

At that moment there was a terrific clap of thunder and the giant waited until it had died away before he spoke again. "I take you to doctor. Come."

"But I only . . ."

His arm was seized by a gigantic hand and he was pulled toward the door, while his loudly proclaimed objections were completely ignored. They went back across the hall, along another long passage, down a flight of steps, and finally entered a small basement room that appeared to be situated at the back of the house. It was furnished with two armchairs, a long bench under the window, and a battered desk. Behind the desk sat a little white-haired man, whose small blue eyes were magnified by a large pair of spectacles. He looked up as Rodney was pulled into the room and expressed his astonishment by removing his spectacles, wiping them carefully with a yellow duster, then putting them on again. He spoke in a rather squeaky voice.

"What's the meaning of this, Daniel? Who is this boy?"

Clearly Daniel did not believe in wasting words.

"Found him upstairs."

The little man raised his eyebrows.

"Found him upstairs! 'Pon my soul! This won't do at all. You know very well, Daniel, my work is reaching a crucial stage and I mustn't be disturbed."

"Been walking about," Daniel stated. "Footsteps in dust."

Rodney thought it was about time that he again explained the situation. "I thought the house was empty, sir, and as I am wet through . . ."

"Good heavens, so he is!" the little man interrupted. "He's dripping water all over the carpet and must be well on the way to catching cold. Can't have that. The germs might get round and fasten their teeth on Henry."

Daniel shook his head violently. "Doctor Frankwell—boy has ears."

Doctor Frankwell adjusted his spectacles. "So he has. So what? He'd look very funny without them."

"Hear too much," Daniel insisted. "Got mouth. Talk."

Doctor Frankwell sighed deeply. "Oh, dear! I keep forgetting not to mention Henry. Now look here, boy, you will forget that I ever did. There's no such person.

You will dismiss the name of Henry completely from your mind. Is that clear?"

Rodney, who was really very wet and extremely cold into the bargain, and would have been quite willing to forget his own name for some dry clothes, said: "Yes, sir. Now, can you please . . ."

The doctor waved his hand impatiently. "Yes . . . yes. Take him away, Daniel, and dry him out. Better give him something to eat afterward, but don't let him near Hen . . . I mean, near anyone."

Daniel did not bother to use any more words, he just pulled Rodney out of the room, pushed him along the passage, and deposited him in a bedroom. He opened a chest of drawers and took out a pair of trousers and a thick woolen pullover. "Put on," he instructed. "Bring wet clothes to kitchen. First door on right." Then he went out and Rodney heard his heavy footsteps recede down the passage.

The trousers and pullover must have been the property of Doctor Frankwell, because they were a very tight fit, but they were at least warm and dry, so it was with a lighter heart—and a fully aroused curiosity—that Rodney emerged from the bedroom and made his way toward the first door on the right.

The kitchen was in a mess. Unwashed plates and saucepans were piled on the wooden draining board, the sink was full of cold, greasy water, and the floor was simply littered with turnip tops, potato peelings, and screwed-up paper bags. When Rodney entered, Daniel was examining a half-cooked leg of lamb that he had just removed from the old-fashioned iron range. He pointed to a large wooden chair.

"Hang clothes on back. Put in front of fire."

Rodney draped his trousers over the chair back, and laid his shirt, underpants, and socks across the seat. Then he watched Daniel's culinary activities.

The huge man was cutting off the red, juicy parts of the joint, but the deeper he cut, the more it became obvious that the meat was under-cooked.

"Excuse me . . ." Rodney, who had taken a cookery course in the Scouts, had to speak up. "I think you have taken it out of the oven too soon."

Daniel said: "Ugh"—or a sound to that effect—and stared at the leg of lamb with an air of complete helplessness.

"May I help you?" asked Rodney.

Daniel started as though he had been stung by a wasp. "Help?"

"Yes, I can cook. And, since you and the doctor have been so kind—I'll be pleased to—well—clear up for you."

Daniel looked slowly around the kitchen. "Clear up? Nothing want clearing up."

"Nonsense!" Rodney could not restrain his indignation. "This place is in an awful mess. Where is the broom?"

"Broom?"

Eventually Rodney found some cleaning materials in a narrow cupboard and set to work while Daniel watched him with growing approval. Presently the leg of lamb, surrounded by a circle of potatoes, still attired in their brown jackets, was back in the oven, a saucepan of Brussels sprouts was simmering on the hotplate, and the kitchen floor had been cleared of all refuse.

"Perhaps," Rodney suggested, "you will give me a hand with the washing up."

"Washing up?"

"Yes. All these dirty plates and things. They need washing."

"Only get dirty again."

Daniel was finally prevailed upon to dry up, but he wasn't very good at it, because at least three plates crashed to the floor and one cup lost its handle.

"What does the doctor do?" Rodney asked, assuming an air of casualness.

"He—make things."

"Oh, really? I thought doctors treated sick people and wrote out prescriptions."

This was a bit too much for Daniel and he frowned as though his slow-working brain was struggling with a very complicated problem. At last he spoke.

"Must not talk about what doctor do. It's se-se—"

"Secret?" Rodney suggested. "I say, is he working for the government?"

Daniel frowned again. "No gov-er-ment. No talk. Se-cret."

But Rodney did not give up so easily. "I expect you are a great help. The doctor is very lucky to have such an intelligent person to rely on."

Daniel thought about this for some time, then his lips parted to reveal large, fearsome-looking teeth.

"I am big help. The doctor let me shift big pieces on to table and once . . . You not tell him I tell you this?"

"Oh, no."

"Well," and an expression of almost childish pride transformed Daniel's face, "once I pulled big switch and made all the lights jump along wires."

"Gosh!" Rodney displayed all the signs of suitable admiration. "You are clever. What happened?"

Daniel sighed very deeply. "No good. All the pieces flew apart. Doctor start again. But this time . . ."

He stopped, looked suspiciously at Rodney, then shook his head. "I not talk anymore. Nobody must know. You help get dinner ready."

Dinner was served in a small dining room that was situated on the opposite side of the passage to the kitchen. Rodney laid the table and Daniel brought in the by-now succulent joint, then went to fetch the doctor. The little man came bustling in and positively beamed when he saw the sizzling lamb, the crisp potatoes, and the steaming Brussels sprouts.

"'Pon my soul! Daniel, you have excelled yourself. Absolutely excelled yourself."

Daniel tried to assume a modest expression but was quite unable to suppress a self-satisfied grin.

"Boy helped," he admitted with some reluctance.

"Did he now?" Doctor Frankwell seated himself at the head of the table and began to carve the lamb as though he were performing some intricate operation. "What a bright lad he is, to be sure. Daniel, after dinner I will require your help. Henry has been lapping up the electricity all day . . ."

Daniel made a sound that was halfway between a cough and a growl and jerked his head in the direction of Rodney. The doctor gasped.

"Oh dear, I've done it again. Lad, do you realize there is no such person as Henry? As for lapping up electricity—he never did. Never. I mean to say—he couldn't—could he?"

"No, sir," Rodney agreed.

"That's all right then. I can't imagine what came over me, talking such rubbish. Nevertheless, Daniel, I think it would be safe to say, tonight you will be able to pull the big switch."

For a moment it seemed as if Daniel would get up and do a little dance. But he contented himself with banging a spoon on the table instead.

"Pu-ll the big switch! And all the lights will jump along wires?"

Doctor Frankwell nodded violently. "No doubt of it. Henry will be up and about . . . Boy, you must have some more Brussels sprouts. Very good for you . . ."

A dramatic interruption cut short his words. From somewhere a little way off came the sound of a loud thud, followed by the tinkle of broken glass. The doctor jumped to his feet.

"Goodness gracious. Daniel—quickly, man, he's fallen off the table."

He rushed from the room, closely followed by Daniel, turned left and went running down the passage. At first Rodney decided that whatever was taking place was no business of his, but he was soon creeping down the passage, making his way toward an open door at the far end.

He entered a large room that had probably been a larder at one time, for there were long slate shelves lining the walls and a massive table running down the center. Rodney noted the electrical equipment that stood on shelves, was screwed into the ceiling, and sent coils of copper wire to the table. But his full attention was drawn toward Doctor Frankwell—and the *thing* that lay on the floor. It was approximately seven feet long; a grotesque human shape, swathed in a green plastic sheet, and it had various colored sockets jutting out from the head, chest, and ribs. The doctor was fussing about like an old hen whose chick had gone astray.

"Careful, Daniel. He may have loosened something. Gently, man."

Daniel lifted the huge figure and laid it reverently on the table, then stood to one side as Doctor Frankwell fitted wires to the sockets and made adjustments to a dial that was strapped across the stomach.

"No damage done, Daniel. We did our work well. He's fully charged, and when you pull the big switch he'll be up and about."

"Boy here," Daniel pointed out. "He see all."

The doctor spun round and there was a most pathetic expression on his face. "Oh, dear! Now the same thing will happen to me, that ruined the work of my great-great-grandfather—the famous Baron Frankenstein. He left the door of his laboratory open and a little girl called Mary Wollstonecraft Godwin got in and later wrote a full account of what she saw—the little beast—that was read by the entire world. I hope you are not addicted to pen and paper, young fellow."

"Oh no," Rodney hastened to reassure the little man. "I hate writing. But have you really created a monster?"

"Most certainly not." Doctor Frankwell looked as indignant as his mild features would allow. "I have designed, manufactured, and will shortly activate a Humanoid-Electronic-Non-lethal-Rapid-developer-Youngster. Henry for short."

"Good heavens!" Rodney could not tear his fascinated gaze away from the shape on the table. "Did you make it out of . . . dead bodies?"

The doctor laughed gently. "Times have changed and we have progressed since the days of my late lamented great-great-grandfather. I have used a special self-adhesive plastic, some blood substitute fluid that I have called GFI, and an awful lot of electricity."

"Now boy know everything," Daniel pointed out.

"Yes, but what does it matter?" The doctor took his spectacles off, wiped them on a corner of Henry's sheet, then replaced them. "As soon as Henry is up and about, the entire world will know. Can't you see the headlines? *Doctor Frankwell Creates a Man*. I expect I'll be invited to appear on television."

"Shall I pull big switch now?" Daniel asked.

"Well . . ." the doctor looked undecided until Rodney reminded him of a very important fact.

"We haven't finished our dinner yet."

The doctor's spectacles slipped down his nose and his eyes widened with shocked horror. "Great Scott, you're right! And the roast lamb will be getting cold."

They all but ran back to the dining-room and continued their interrupted meal, although the doctor kept
jumping up and trotting to his laboratory to make sure
that Henry had not fallen off the table again. At length,
knives and forks were laid aside, plates were stacked
and carried into the kitchen, and Doctor Frankwell
beamed at his assistant.

"Daniel—I can think of no reason for further delay.
Henry is fully charged, his working parts are in excellent condition—the great moment has arrived."

Henry certainly appeared to be very lively, if the strange
twitching movement that was taking place in every part of
the shrouded figure was any criterion. Doctor Frankwell
first of all made sure that all the wires were fully connected
to the sockets, then turned his head and nodded to Daniel,
who was standing by a very large wall switch.

"Now," he said.

Daniel pulled the lever. Instantly, pulsating streamers of colored light ran along the wires; electric bulbs
lit up and flashed on and off like neon signs, and from
the far comer of the room a large metal box began to
make a loud buzzing sound.

Henry displayed every sign of being well and truly
activated. The huge shape was writhing like a cut
worm; the sheet-covered head rolled from side to side,
and there seemed a distinct possibility that the entire
bundle would roll down on to the floor again.

"Daniel!" Doctor Frankwell shouted, his voice shrill with excitement. "Watch him. I am going to increase the current. It's do or burst!"

Rodney sincerely hoped Henry would not burst. On the other hand, he was not at all sure that he wanted to see a homemade monster walk, either. He seemed to remember that the one created by Baron Frankenstein had not behaved in a civilized manner. He watched the doctor turning knobs, pressing different colored buttons, all of which resulted in the wires becoming brighter, the bulbs flashing more quickly, and the buzzing sound rising to an earsplitting shriek.

Suddenly there was a loud bang and all the lights went out. The wires became dull black, the electric bulbs went pop-pop, one after the other, and the metal box that had been making the awful noise became as silent as a Quaker's meeting. And Henry? After the doctor had lit three candles, it was easy to see there was no sign of life.

"All the wires are burnt out," the little doctor sighed deeply. "Three years' work gone up in puffs of smoke."

"Perhaps the fuses want mending," Rodney suggested, surprised to realize that he was disappointed that Henry was not going to walk. But Doctor Frankwell shook his head.

"No, all my equipment is ruined. I overloaded it, you see."

"I put kettle on," Daniel stated. "Make tea."

The doctor smiled bravely. "Well, I suppose we might feel better after a cup of tea. There's not much we can do here."

They adjourned to the kitchen where Daniel placed a large iron kettle on the hotplate, then brewed some really excellent tea in a brown pot. There was no doubt that the doctor enjoyed his cup, for he sipped it with every sign of appreciation and had quite recovered from his disappointment after a second one.

"It's back to the drawing board, Daniel. We must use stouter wiring, double the feedbacks, and install an even bigger switch."

Daniel said, "Ugh," but did not seem all that keen.

"In the meanwhile," the doctor went on, "we might as well get some rest. I dare say we can find our young friend a bed?"

Daniel nodded and poured some of his tea into a saucer.

Rodney was about to express his gratitude when his ears detected a slight sound. A very slow slithering, followed by the creak of protesting floorboards. Daniel also heard it, for his head came up, then turned in the direction of the open doorway.

No one spoke. They just sat, waiting for the impossible to put in an appearance. Now the slithering was alternating with loud thuds. Slither-thud-slither-thud, and the suspense was so intense that Rodney dropped his cup. Then something very large filled the doorway. Still swathed in a plastic sheet, with bits of wire dangling from the colored sockets, with the dial still strapped to its stomach, the Humanoid-Electronic-Non-lethal-Rapid-developer-Youngster lurched into the room and stood swaying like a tall tree in a hundred-mile-per-hour gale. Doctor Frankwell was the first to speak.

"It did work, Daniel! We gave up too soon. Henry is up and about."

The plastic sheet bulged as two great hands came out and pushed against the confining material. Rodney heard a tearing sound as a long, ragged hole appeared, and one immense and one smaller fist sprang into view and began to punch the air in a most aggressive fashion.

"I don't think he likes us very much," Rodney gasped.

"Nonsense." Doctor Frankwell adjusted his spectacles. "He's just pleased to be alive. Daniel, get him unwrapped. Be careful you don't hurt him."

Daniel displayed praiseworthy caution. He approached the monster from the rear and unzipped a long fastener that ran from the top of the swaying head down to the gigantic feet. The sheet fell away, and it took all of Rodney's self-control not to turn tail and race from the room.

Henry was not at all pretty. A head that resembled
a misshapen turnip was surmounted by a mop of red
hair. One eye was blue and round, the other brown and
slanted. The mouth was extremely wide and filled with
large, yellow teeth. The nose could have been mistaken
for a parrot's beak, the ears for the wings of an ancient
bat. A mighty chest was flanked by arms of unequal
length. Rodney could not see the legs, for the creature
was dressed in a long, flannel nightgown, but the feet
had much in common with two overturned vegetable
dishes.

Doctor Frankwell beamed his delight and was
clearly waiting for everyone's unstinted admiration.
"Well—what do you think of him?"

It took a few seconds for Rodney to regain his power
of speech.

"He's—he's not very handsome—is he?"

"Not handsome!" The doctor frowned, then examined his creation with some anxiety. "How can you say
that? Why—he's positively beautiful. Possibly I could
have taken a little more care in the matter of his arms
and eyes, but I think that a little irregularity of features can be quite attractive. Daniel, let's get him into
a chair and invite him to take some nourishment."

Getting Henry to sit down was not all that easy. He
took a wide swing at Daniel, then resisted most forcibly
when that person exerted all his strength and pushed

him into the doctor's chair. The little man looked at the remains of the leg of lamb and cold baked potatoes. "Do you think we should cook him something special, Daniel? Perhaps we could tempt him with a nice steak and kidney pie."

Henry literally took matters into his own hands. The round eye stared at the cold lamb, the slanted one examined the potatoes. Apparently the round eye won the decision. The larger fist grabbed, the smaller one tore, and the great teeth began to munch. Perhaps *crunch* would be a better word, because Henry was not a dainty eater. Meat, bones—all went into the gaping mouth, were crushed and swallowed in a little under five seconds. The doctor was delighted by this display of rapid consumption.

"He's got a healthy appetite. Gracious, Daniel, if this keeps up, he'll eat us."

Rodney thought this more than likely and decided he would not like to be around when the supply of roast lamb ran out. Having eaten, Henry slept. First the slanted eye closed, then the round one—having swiveled in its socket as though to make sure all was well—also lowered its lid, and for a while there was peace. Then the wide mouth opened and a sound that was rather like a saw being driven through a hard piece of wood filled the kitchen. Henry not only slept—he snored.

The doctor yawned and Daniel rubbed his eyes.

"Well, Henry has set us a good example. Time we were all in bed. Daniel, do you suppose he will be comfortable there?"

"Not like to wake up," replied Daniel, with obvious deep sincerity. "If he not comfortable, can go back to lab-ora-tory."

The doctor rose. "Yes, you are right. Leave the door open for him."

As Rodney was taken upstairs and installed in a little dust-haunted room on the ground floor, he could not help wondering if it was wise to leave Henry all by himself. After some reflection he barricaded his door by wedging a chair-back under the handle, then lay down on top of the bed fully clothed.

The old house was very quiet. The storm had long ago exhausted its rage and gone to sleep in the western sky. A full moon peered in through the undraped window and tinted the old furniture with silver light, forcing black slabs of shadow to lurk in corners and take on weird shapes. Rodney tried to keep awake, but what with one thing and another (he had had a tiring day), unconsciousness crept up on him like a soft-footed burglar.

He was awakened by a crash. He lay perfectly still for some time, his heart thudding wildly, trying to dismiss the chilling thought that Henry was up and around. After a few minutes he heard the sound of disturbed broken glass, followed by a low wail that could have been made by an abandoned dog—or by a homemade monster that is not exactly dancing for joy.

Curiosity and fear fought a hard battle. Curiosity—after much serious thought—won. Rodney crept to the door, removed the chair, then went out into the passage. The clatter of broken glass drew him toward a room that was situated a few yards away. Rodney saw the by-now-familiar neglect, the dust—and the smashed mirror that was scattered over the floor, each separate particle reflecting the bright moonlight, making them gleam like fallen stars. Henry was slumped against the wall, his grotesque face masked by shadow, his ridiculous hands held out as though in supplication. Rodney felt his fear ebb away as he advanced into the room, dimly realizing that Henry might be a monster, something designed and manufactured by Doctor Frankwell, but apparently he also had emotions. Was unhappy.

"What's the matter?" he asked, not that there was much hope that Henry would understand him, although the *R* in his name did stand for *Rapid-developer*.

The ungainly figure came out into the moonlight, the right hand pointing to the broken shards of mirror-glass, and a strangled sound escaped from the wide mouth. Rodney picked up the largest piece of glass and stared at it thoughtfully. He held it out and Henry shrank back with a muted cry.

"It won't hurt you. It was only an old mirror, and I don't suppose the doctor will be angry that you broke it. He doesn't appear to use this part of the house."

Henry's large hand came out, pointed to the piece of mirror, then turned and indicated his own face. Understanding flooded Rodney's mind with an all-revealing light.

"You saw a reflection! It frightened you! Gosh, I expect it would. Look—that was you. See?"

He held the piece of mirror above his head and tilted it until his own young face was reflected in the gleaming surface; then turned until it could be seen by the monster. Henry snatched the fragment of glass from him and stared at it intently. Suddenly he pointed to himself and made a growling sound.

Rodney nodded violently. "You. It's you—nothing to be frightened of."

Henry did not appear to be comforted by this information. He flung the piece of glass across the room and Rodney was surprised to see a solitary tear trickle down from the large eye, while a little moaning cry seeped out from between the sagging lips. He crashed both hands together and uttered his first word.

"Ye-e-w . . ."

Rodney nodded again. "It should be me, but you seem to have got the point. I say, you are bright."

Henry lurched forward. Taking long floor-shaking steps, he crossed the room and moved slowly into the passage, with Rodney following a few yards behind. Boy and monster descended the stairs to the basement, and here Henry continued to advance until he reached the laboratory door. A single push from his right fist sent it hurtling back and a terrible suspicion flared up in Rodney's brain.

He called out: "Doctor . . . Daniel . . . come quickly!"

The doctor emerged from a room on the left, dressed in a long white nightgown and wearing a tasseled nightcap. He hurriedly put on his spectacles and peered at Rodney with some irritation.

"Gracious me, what is all this noise about? I must have my eight-hours sleep. Absolutely essential."

"It's Henry." Rodney explained. "He saw his own reflection, and now I think he's going to do something awful."

As though to confirm his words, there came from the laboratory a mighty crashing and thumping; a splintering of wood, a shattering of glass, all intermingled with loud roars of insensate rage.

"What on earth has come over him?" the doctor asked, by now looking extremely agitated. "Heavens above, he's ruining all my equipment. I will never be able to replace it. Daniel!"

Daniel appeared from another room, looking rather ridiculous in a woolen vest and a long pair of underpants. He ruffled his hair, rubbed his eyes, then asked:

"What's wrong? Somebody making noise."

The doctor waved his hands frantically in the direction of the laboratory. "Henry's gone berserk. Get in there and restrain him."

Daniel did not seem all that keen to obey this last instruction, but he dutifully went toward the laboratory, with the doctor and Rodney walking cautiously in his footsteps. When he reached the doorway, he stopped and motioned his employer forward.

"All finished," he said simply.

Rodney looked fearfully over Doctor Frankwell's shoulder and came to an immediate decision that Henry had done a thorough job. All the intricate equipment had been smashed, broken wires hung like dead snakes from walls and ceiling, and even the table had been shattered into jagged fragments. Only one item still remained intact, and that was the large metal box that had formerly given out a loud, buzzing noise. Henry was working on that now. He had it raised high above his head and was about to crash it down on to the floor.

"Stop him!" the doctor shouted. "That is my charger. Thousands of volts of electricity are stored in there. The slightest jar and Henry will be blown to smithereens."

Everyone began shouting at once, trying to explain
to Henry his predicament. He stood perfectly still,
the charger clutched in his ill-assorted hands, and it
seemed to Rodney that a light of dawning understanding gleamed in the round, large eye.

"That," the doctor said, pointing to the box, "bang
when you drop. You—" He spread wide his hands.
"—Finished. Over. Dead. No more."

Seconds passed, then Henry's mouth opened and he
uttered two more words. "Ye-e-w fin-ish-ed?"

The doctor nodded. Daniel nodded. Rodney closed
his eyes and dramatically pretended he was about to fall
down. Henry seemed to get the message, for he nodded,
too. When Daniel made a slight movement forward,
though, he growled warningly. The doctor sighed.

"Perhaps we had better leave him alone. Come to
think of it, we would be in great danger should he drop
that charger."

Rodney felt very sad as they trailed back along the
passage, then took refuge on the stairs and waited
for what they all knew must happen. The explosion
was not very loud, just a muted booming noise, followed by a flash of bright light. The doctor and Daniel
went back into the devastated laboratory, but Rodney
remained on the stairs. Presently the two men came
back. The doctor was dabbing at his eyes with a large
pocket-handkerchief.

"Nothing left," he said. "All my work gone up in a flash. I will never have the heart to start again."

"Make hair restorer," Daniel suggested. "Lots of men bald. Me bald."

Doctor Frankwell, suddenly, looked much happier.

"I say, that's not a bad idea. Make some money, too. Then I'll be able to get this place done up. Thank you, Daniel."

Daniel grinned delightedly and produced another gem of wisdom.

"Make hair—not men."

Later, when Rodney was cycling down a country lane, far away from that house of dust-coated furniture, he felt glad that Henry was no more. After all, there are enough monsters in the world, without homemade ones.

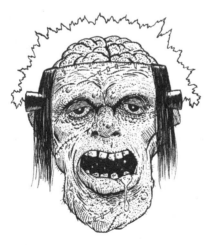

THE SIDEWAYS LADY
Lynda E. Rucker

A FAMILY VANISHED, sixty years after the house's previous occupants died under mysterious circumstances. An old house of ancient, unknown, and perhaps evil provenance. A specter known only, enigmatically, as "The Sideways Lady," and a small town, caught in the grip of terror for more than a hundred years . . .

Toby said, "We aren't gripped by terror."

"Shut up," Stevie said. She went on reading . . .

What is known today as the Beaumont House was disassembled in England, brought to the small town of Ellington, Virginia, in the United States, and reassembled by a man who made his fortune in the railways around the turn of the twentieth century. His beloved wife wanted to live in a castle. The Beaumont House is not quite a castle, but it was then and still is today the biggest, most ostentatious house in town.

Toby asked, "What's ostentatious?"
"Fancy."

At first the railway man and his wife entertained often at the house, holiday events that the whole town was invited to, parties, even a few balls. But after a year or so, and quite suddenly, everything stopped. The house was closed up; the man and his wife rarely left, and the next anyone heard of them, they were both found dead in the house of unknown causes.

"What does that mean?" Toby asked again.
"It means they don't know what killed them."
"Rabies?" Toby suggested.
He was obsessed with rabies these days, having seen something about it online, or in school.
"People don't just *come down* with rabies, Toby. It's not like getting a cold. Now stop interrupting and let me finish reading you this."

The house stayed closed up for over sixty years, sinking into its own decay. But in the months before the arrival of the Beaumonts, in the late 1960s, it hummed with life again, workmen reviving and restoring the place. When the Beaumont family arrived, mother, father, and three teenage children, it seemed at first as though the place might truly return to its old, if brief, glory. Nat Beaumont was a state senator with a promising political career ahead of him—some said he'd be governor within a few years. His wife, Thelma, had been a teacher before marrying him and having children, and like the first couple who lived there, they opened the house up to parties and celebrations.

But after a few months, the strangeness started again. People said Kathleen Beaumont, the oldest of the three teenagers, was behaving oddly. She told her friends at school that someone called the "Sideways Lady" had come to live in her house. One of her schoolmates reported that when a teacher reprimanded her for falling asleep in class, she said the Sideways Lady kept waking her up by trying to get into her bed.

Not long after that, Kathleen's parents pulled her out of school completely. They mentioned to a few people that they were taking her to see doctors, but the town went wild with rumors. Her friends said she claimed to have summoned a demon, and the story was that the family sought a priest to come in to exorcise, although the local clergy denied any knowledge of such a thing.

And then, on Halloween night, 1969, the entire family went missing.

There were no signs of violence or foul play. There was no sign of anything at all. Luggage, purses, money, identification, keys—anything you might take if you went on the run were left behind, plus there was no whiff of scandal that would have caused the family to take such a drastic step.

The focus of law enforcement fell on the missing Nat Beaumont all the same, but despite a nation-wide search, no trace of him or his family was ever found.

In Ellington it was different. The rumors grew over the years that Kathleen had murdered them all: her parents and her younger brother and sister, Hugh and Sarah. But she was gone like the rest of them.

Many say now that Kathleen's demon-ridden spirit haunts the abandoned Beaumont House, luring unwary passersby to the same doom she took her family to.

For now, it seems, the truth about the Beaumont House remains unknown unless True Hauntings decides to pay it a visit and unearth its secrets once and for all!

Got a tip about a haunted house in your town? Send us the story, and maybe we'll feature it on our website. We might even do a True Hauntings *show about it! Thanks to Hannah B. for sending us this one, and remember, stay spooky!*

Toby said, "That show is dumb. It isn't real."

Stevie tried not to show her little brother how exasperated she was with him. "But it's our favorite!"

"It's *your* favorite."

"We can go check out the house and maybe send something about it to them, and maybe they'll come and investigate it. Wouldn't that be cool? Maybe they'd even put us on the show!"

"If the stuff they say about ghosts in that show is real," Toby said, "how come Mom never tries to contact us?"

Stevie, who had been kneeling in front of him pasting cutout stars on the old overcoat he wore—a wizard's cloak, she assured him—sat back on her heels. "Because," she replied. "Mom is at peace. Ghosts haunt places because they aren't at peace. Mom's sad she left us, but she knows we're okay so she doesn't have to do any haunting. Anyway, she said she'd always be with us. Remember what she told us: *Look for me in the moonlight and on the wind.* And when we look up at the moon tonight we can think about her watching us." She handed him a stick with shredded yellow and orange construction paper taped on the end of it. "There's your wizard's wand."

Toby looked at it dubiously. "I don't get it."

"It's flames coming out of the wand!" She gave him a hug. "You look like a powerful magician," she said. "It's an awesome costume." What he looked like really was a sad, anxious little boy swallowed up by his father's cast-off overcoat.

She felt she'd betrayed her mother because she didn't dress up this year like she had at her old school, in the witch costume her mother had made her when she was Toby's age and altered every year as she grew. She'd overheard kids saying twelve was too old to dress up for Halloween. It was hard, being the new kid in a new school, a new town. Of course, as it turned out, half of those kids *did* dress up after all. She'd sat through math, social studies, and science surrounded by zombies and cats and vampires and superheroes, feeling human and vulnerable.

Halloween is witchy.

That's what their mother used to say. She had loved Halloween. For weeks beforehand, the house would be draped in orange and black. A skeleton might take up residence in the rocking chair before a front window.

Fake tombstones sprouted in the front yard with funny epitaphs she took from a book by a man named Edward Gorey. *G is for George smothered under a rug.* Last year, the day after Halloween, some parents had come to talk to her. Apparently she'd gone too far, frightened their children. She'd had to invite the kids over for something innocuous, something ridiculous, cookies and Kool-Aid and showing them around, showing that it wasn't really a Witch House and that nothing bad could hurt them. Stevie had never seen her mother as exhausted as she'd been at the end of that day. "No wonder I don't hang out with the other parents," she had said, tucked up in bed while Stevie brought her cups of tea. "God, they're boring. Are they all like that?"

"Pretty much," Stevie replied. It was the reason she didn't have a lot of friends either. That never bothered her, until her mother died and she and Toby had to leave the "Witch House" and their old town and everything from her old life behind, and she went from few friends to no friends in the new place.

"Let's make a deal," she said to Toby now. "I'll take you trick-or-treating, and when we're done we'll walk over to the Beaumont House. If you think it's too weird or scary we won't go inside, we'll just look at it from the outside."

Toby still looked doubtful.

She leaned in close to him and whispered in his ear in a silly, growly voice. "We won't stop until we have *all the candy!*" He giggled, and she said it again. *"Alllllll the candy!"*

"Okay," he agreed, still giggling.

"Okay," she said. "Wait here. I gotta get dressed. And then we'll eat something and we'll go."

Her witch dress was too short and too tight, but Stevie didn't know how to sew or how to find someone who did to fix it. She guessed it was the last year she'd be wearing it. She could fit into it, barely, but it was kind of hard to breathe. *Magic in every stitch of it,* that's what her mother always said. *For my witchy baby girl.*

Stevie was making them hot dogs for dinner when their dad came in from work. Living with him was weird, like living with a stranger—which he was, a distant figure they only saw a couple times a year until suddenly they had to move in with him. He tried, she'd give him that. Every once in a while he turned up with a pizza and a clutch of Blu-rays, announcing it was "Family Night!" They took dutiful part. The movies were usually too young for either of them. Their father always fell asleep before they were over.

He looked faintly surprised to see them there in the kitchen, as he often did, like he'd forgotten he had children. Stevie said, "Hi, Dad. Want me to make you a hot dog?"

He shook his head. "What are you kids up to tonight?"

"I'm taking Toby out trick-or-treating."

"Well, don't be late." He opened the fridge, stared in it for a while, and then closed it again without taking anything out. "And be careful," he added as he left the room, like he remembered those were the kinds of things dads were supposed to say.

The moon was nearly full and peeking at them through the black branches of trees as they headed out. They passed a gaggle of Harry Potter characters and several princesses.

"All of these houses have their lights on, why aren't we stopping?" Toby asked.

"There are better houses further on," Stevie said. She wanted to get away from their neighbors, go to some streets where nobody knew who they were and would answer the door without that expression that said *it's those poor children with the dead mother.* Where they could just be regular kids. She also wanted to keep them moving in the direction of the Beaumont House, which was a couple of miles' walk away, kind of far for Toby, but she hoped that the trick-or-treating would distract him.

"My bag's too heavy," he said eventually.

She poured half of it into her bag and handed it back to him.

"Now *you* have all the candy!"

"You can have it all when we get home."

"My feet hurt."

The moon scudded behind clouds and they found themselves walking through an older part of town with no streetlights. Just as Toby started in with, "I don't care about the haunted house any longer, I want to go home," they were there.

Stevie had not been able to find any photos of the Beaumont House online, but what they saw before them was better than her imagination. Set back from the road, surrounded by an iron gate, a dark and dilapidated form against a darker October sky. She and Toby stood there for a moment.

"I don't like it," Toby said. "Let's go home."

"It's haunted, you know," came a voice from behind them.

Kids from school: Stevie recognized them, a set of twins, a boy and a girl. They were both tall and pale with short dark hair, and tonight they were wearing black jeans and black hoodies.

"Are you guys urbexers too?" the girl asked. Stevie remembered her name then. Taylor. And her brother was Tristan.

"What's an urbexer?"

"Urban explorer," Tristan replied. "We explore abandoned places."

"We just came to see the haunted house," Stevie said.

"That makes you an urbexer. As long as you do it right," explained Tristan.

"What's doing it right?"

"Stay calm. Don't mess with anything. Leave it the way you found it. Don't get caught."

"That was the plan," Stevie said. "But I'm not an urban explorer. I'm a ghost-hunter."

Taylor said, "We've never explored a place that was supposed to be haunted before."

Four seemed like a lot for a ghost hunt. If you had too many people, the ghosts probably wouldn't show themselves. That was why you never heard about ghosts turning up in, say, football stadiums, or malls.

On the other hand, as the saying went, there was safety in numbers.

Stevie said, "You know that show, *True Hauntings*? They might come here and investigate it. I'm checking it out for them."

"Why would they hire a kid?" asked Tristan.

"It's not like a hiring thing," Stevie said. "It's like a consultant."

"I don't believe you," Taylor said.

"Anyway, that show's about fake stuff," Tristan added. "This isn't fake. Our grandmother knew that girl. Kathleen Beaumont. They were friends. She remembers when it all happened."

"What does she think happened to them?"

"She said she didn't think Kathleen would hurt anybody."

"What about that Sideways Lady?"

Taylor spoke up, "I knew someone who saw her once."

"Really?"

Taylor nodded solemnly. "She said it was terrifying, what she did."

Stevie was almost too afraid to ask. "What was it?"

"She—" Taylor stopped. "*She stood sideways.*"

"Don't be mean, Taylor," Tristan admonished, but Stevie was embarrassed. The evening was going to ruin. She wanted to take Toby and go home, but she didn't want them—Taylor especially—to think she was a coward.

The four of them stood and looked at the house before them. Stevie had the feeling that the house stared back, that its blank windows were eyes.

Stevie and Toby stashed their bags of Halloween candy in the bushes—Taylor and Tristan didn't have any—and picked their way across the overgrown yard. The closer they got to the house, the tighter a little ball in Stevie's stomach curled.

Tristan whispered, "Did you bring flashlights?"

She shook her head.

"First rule of urbexing is you should always be prepared," Tristan explained, and pressed one into her hand. "Don't you have any ghost-hunting equipment?"

Kev and Lori, the hosts on *True Hauntings*, always went prepared. Stevie hadn't even thought about how they were going to get into the house.

That, at least, did not seem to be a problem. As they stepped up onto the porch, she could see that the front door was slightly ajar.

Stevie hung back and let Tristan and Taylor go in first before following behind, holding Toby's hand tightly. They played their flashlight beams along the ceiling, the walls. They were standing in an empty foyer, a hallway that disappeared into darkness, doors on either side, a stairway in front of them. Wallpaper hung in strips. She couldn't discern the pattern, but it made her shudder all the same because it suddenly made her think of flayed skin. What if houses were like people? What if they hurt, what if they were full of all these complicated emotions that people carried inside them?

What would happen if you opened a door and let those feelings *out*?

Taylor whispered, "Let's go upstairs."

And then someone said, "What are you children doing in my house?"

The woman staring at them, holding a lantern up next to a wrinkled face framed by wild white hair, was wearing a white, high-necked, old-fashioned nightgown. Her feet were bare. She must have come through one of the closed doors in the hallway that stretched before them into darkness, but they could not see which one.

For a long moment, none of them said a word. Then the woman continued, "If you've come here to steal from me, I don't have any money. There's nothing here to take."

"Oh!" Stevie didn't know she was going to make a noise until it was out. She was horrified that the woman thought they were thieves. "No! We—thought nobody lived here."

"Nobody does," the woman said. "I'm nobody."

Taylor asked, "Are you Kathleen Beaumont?"

"That name sounds familiar," the woman replied. "But I don't think I've ever had a name."

Stevie said, "We're very sorry. We'll go."

"You can't go yet," the woman responded. "It's Halloween night, is that right? Come and sit with me. I have some cakes I can give you. That's what you want on Halloween, isn't it? Sweets?" She smiled, but when she did, her grin reminded Stevie of the wolf in a fairy tale, a mouth stretched back from long canine teeth.

Stevie said quickly, "No, we—"

"I'm so lonely," the woman continued. "No one ever comes to see me. Now I have my own little witch and little wizard visitors, and even they don't want to stay."

Stevie remembered that they were supposed to be ghost-hunters. When you were a ghost-hunter, when somebody invited you further into a haunted house, you weren't supposed to say *no*.

They followed the woman into a room off the foyer. It had been a grand room once, you could tell, but now it was empty save for a crumbling fireplace, a chandelier that had fallen at some point and been placed in a corner, and dozens of candles the woman had lit and set about on the floor. They had to move carefully to avoid them.

"Wait here, my dears," she said, and there was that horrible parody of a smile again. "I'll be right back," and she went through another doorway.

To Toby, who had never been so quiet, Stevie warned, "Don't eat anything she gives you."

"Well, she's not standing sideways, so aside from her being crazy as hell we're probably okay," Taylor said.

The woman was back faster than Stevie expected, carrying a tray with four small china plates, each with what she guessed was a piece of cake on it. It was hard to tell in the candlelight. The woman passed them out and they all stood there awkwardly, holding them. Stevie finally thought of an excuse. "I can't eat gluten," she said. "Neither can my brother."

"What, dearie?"

"I'm so sorry," Stevie said.

"I have no idea what you're talking about," the woman said. "Whatever that is, I'm sure there's none of that nastiness in my cakes."

Taylor asked, "Do you live here alone?"

The woman didn't answer for a while. Then she said, "I think there used to be others here with me. I think I had a family once."

Then Toby blurted out, "Did you kill your family?"

Stevie hissed, "*Toby*!"

But the woman turned her gaze on him. She looked at him for a while, and then smiled her unsettling smile.

"I believe I may have," she said. "Chop, chop, chop, into little pieces."

Toby gaped.

"I'm only teasing, honey! I can't remember, but I think they made up stories about me. You know how small towns are. It was such a long time ago. Will you excuse me for a moment?" The woman got up and went back through the door she'd come out of. The children sat frozen for a moment, then Stevie looked at her cake.

"Guys," she said.

The cakes, they could now see, were black lumps of mold. A terrible smell came off them, and Stevie saw something white moving on hers. *Maggots.* She let out a little cry and dropped it. And then, as though a draft had blown through the room—though they felt nothing—the candles extinguished themselves.

They didn't need to discuss their next move. The four children bolted from the room and back into the foyer. Taylor grabbed the door and yanked it. It would not budge.

Tristan tried; they all did.

"You're the ghost-hunter," Tristan said. "What should we do?"

"I'm not really," Stevie admitted. "I just want to be one someday. Really I'm a witch."

"Stop lying," Taylor snapped.

"I'm not. And this is a witch's dress."

"If you're a witch," Tristan said, "could you get us out of this?"

"That," said Taylor, "would be super helpful."

"I don't even know if she's a ghost or not." They were all talking at once now.

"I think she's real. A person."

"I don't think she killed anybody."

"I think she killed everybody."

"I don't know what she is."

"I don't care what she is."

"If she's a ghost she can't hurt us. She's just like a movie that shows you scary things." That was Toby. "That's what our mom used to say about scary movies."

Tristan pointed out, "This isn't a movie."

Everyone talked at once again.

"She's so old, it's not like she can do anything to hurt us."

"She can if she has an axe."

"I bet she's never hurt a fly."

"Who *is* she, anyway? Is it *her?*"

"It might not be her. She might be a demon."

"We could break one of the windows in that room and climb out it."

"*I'm* not going back in there."

Stevie wondered what Kev and Lori, the ghost-hunters, would do, but the worst thing they ever had to contend with was a cold spot in a house or some creepy noises.

Still, it gave her the courage she needed. "I'll do it," she said. "The front door probably swung shut in that breeze and locked. She'll have a key." She turned and shoved the door open that they'd just come through. "Ms. Beaumont!" she called out, and was surprised at how steady her voice sounded. That made her feel even calmer.

Stevie called out again. "Ms. Beaumont!" She went to the other door and pushed it open.

She expected it to be a kitchen of some sort, but it was just another big, dark, empty room. The woman was standing over in the corner by a window. Just standing there, not doing or saying anything. Stevie tried to say her name again, but nothing came out.

She took a few steps into the room and felt the temperature drop. It was just like Kev and Lori talked about on *True Hauntings*. The dark felt solid, like it was pressing in on her chest. It seemed like there was something wrong with the woman—more wrong than anything they'd already observed—but she couldn't put her finger on what the problem was. Stevie found her voice at last and asked, "Are you okay?"

In that moment, the moon must have moved from behind a cloud, because a shaft of moonlight fell through the window and across the figure.

It wasn't the same woman who had welcomed them into the house earlier.

It was a young woman dressed in clothes of some long-ago period, her profile that of a beautiful lady with hair pulled back from a flawless face. But she held herself with a peculiar kind of tension.

And then she turned.

Only one side was the beautiful young woman. The other was a gaping horror. That face, that entire side of her body, had rotted away, an eye in a ruined socket, teeth set in a clacking jaw of bones, a bare ribcage with tattered pieces of flesh and soft tissue hanging from it. All about the figure there was a great darkness. Its eyes fixed on her, and its mouth opened, and it let out a howl that seemed to go on forever. It raised its hands and spread its fingers, five thin, pale, flawless digits and five bony claws.

The thing flew across the room. The mouth opened wider and wider, impossibly wide, as though it would swallow her whole. Stevie's legs didn't work; her voice

didn't work. *I'm a witch*, she thought. *I'm a witch. I'm a witch. Magic in every stitch.*

I'll be with you in the moonlight and the wind.

The world went black.

Someone was crying.

"*Stevie!*" It was Toby's voice. The first thing she saw was his face, hanging over hers. The next was the night sky behind him, and the moon.

Toby burst into tears.

Stevie pushed herself into a sitting position. They were sitting on the sidewalk, just on the other side of the gate from the Beaumont House.

"I saw her," she said. "The Sideways Lady. She's real."

"Whatever you saw, it gave you superhuman strength, or something," Taylor told her.

They all started talking at once again, but from what she could gather, she had come bolting out of the room—"Your feet weren't touching the ground," Toby said—past the foyer where they were gathered, and yanked the door open like it had never been stuck. They had raced across the yard and through the gate when she had collapsed, and they had been trying to revive her for a good ten minutes.

"If you saw the Sideways Lady," Tristan asked, "then who was the woman *we* met in there?"

Stevie's head felt like someone was hitting it over and over with a sledgehammer. "I don't know," she admitted. "Maybe it was her in another form, trying to trick us. Maybe a ghost."

"But ghosts don't get old."

"I don't know what ghosts do," Stevie said.

Toby cried part of the way home because he was so scared and so relieved and the rest of the way home because he'd left his candy behind. Stevie had to promise him she'd get him more candy, and that night she slept on the floor of his room—so he wouldn't be scared, she told herself, but it was really for herself.

She hung her witch's dress in the back of her closet, where she knew it would be safe but she couldn't see it. She wasn't sure she ever wanted to look at it again.

For weeks she often woke, startled, with the sense that someone had just slipped out of her room. Over time, the fear dissipated, though she still slept fitfully. At school, she and Tristan and Taylor avoided each other. She thought Taylor might have said some mean things about her to some of the other kids, because people started ignoring her even more than usual. A few times she tried to write a letter to *True Hauntings*, but she didn't know what to say, and she eventually abandoned the project.

In the spring, a ferocious tornado ripped through town. It took the roof off a gas station and broke some windows at the high school, but it seemed to have a special fury reserved for one place, in particular.

Stevie got a copy of the local newspaper, the *Ellington Herald*, that reported on the destruction. She cut out the relevant article:

ELLINGTON'S GRANDEST HOME IS NO MORE

by Kay Herndon, staff writer

A structure known locally as the Beaumont House, that has stood for more than a hundred years in Ellington and for centuries before that in its original home in the English countryside, received the brunt of yesterday's destructive storm. Winds measuring at over 150 miles per hour tore through town, but it was the Beaumont House that was the focus of the storm's force and much higher winds. Nearby buildings were left undamaged.

The Beaumont House was lived in for fewer than three of its nearly 120 years in Ellington. The short-lived residencies of its two owners and the mysterious circumstances surrounding their deaths or disappearances gave rise to rumors of hauntings.

Real estate agent Heather Woodrow says she attempted to sell or even rent the house several times on behalf of Adam Beaumont, a descendent of the brother of former State Sen. Nathaniel Beaumont, who, along with his family, was last seen at the home in 1968. Woodrow says despite the house's remarkable features and long history, potential buyers were always put off by what they said was a "bad feeling" they got on walk-throughs.

"I never felt anything like that myself," Woodrow acknowledged. "I think they probably heard stories and that influenced how they felt about it when they finally got around to looking at it.

"Still, you'd think some people would believe it was fun to live in a haunted house! I guess it just never found the right buyers."

The Beaumont House was brought to America in 1899 by Ralph Brightman, a railway baron who wanted a "castle" for his wife. It seems likely that if Brightman or his wife had done any research into the house that was nestled deep in the Devon countryside and sold for a pittance to the rich American on the grounds that it be moved but not destroyed, they might have chosen a different dwelling.

According to the local historical society there, the house, which was built in the seventeenth century, had long been the focus of stories about wealthy peers dabbling in occult rites. One old legend in particular concerned an entity known locally as the "Sydewise Lady." Half-woman and half-demon, she lured people with her unearthly beauty before turning to reveal her demonic other half. It was said that many a weary traveler vanished in the vicinity of the house, which had been abandoned for decades by the time Brightman purchased it.

Over the years, there were local efforts from time to time to have the city of Ellington purchase the home and use it for community events, but these plans always stalled.

Now Ellington's peculiar landmark is no more.

Stevie kept the article, folded up in her desk drawer. She went back to the *True Hauntings* website a few times to reread the story there, but she wasn't able to find it again.

A few weeks after the tornado, she rode her bike over to the site of the Beaumont House one Sunday afternoon. A demolition crew had clearly been working to clean up and haul off the debris the storm left behind. Their equipment—a bulldozer, an excavator with a long yellow arm crooked up toward the sky—sat amid neatly stacked piles of rubble. Nothing was left that was recognizable as a house. The storm's fury had been precise and thorough.

All the same, there was something strange in the air where the house had been. An emptiness, as if a void could have a presence and a shape.

Stevie left her bike on the sidewalk and ignored the signage warning her to keep off the property. She stood where she remembered the porch had been, then took a few steps further into the hallway, the room with the candles, and the terrible place where she had seen the Sideways Lady.

Ever since the tornado, a thought had haunted her, and she could not make it go away.

The storm might have destroyed the house, but what if instead of destroying the Sideways Lady along with it, the wind had scattered her far and wide, releasing her from the walls that kept her captured for centuries? What if now the Sideways Lady could be anywhere she wanted to be?

A shadow moved across the sun, and the warm spring day went cold.

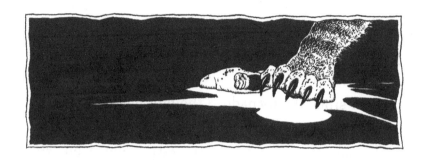

HERE THERE BE TYGERS
STEPHEN KING

CHARLES NEEDED TO go to the bathroom very badly. There was no longer any use in trying to fool himself that he could wait for recess. His bladder was screaming at him, and Miss Bird had caught him squirming.

There were three third-grade teachers in the Acorn Street Grammar School. Miss Kinney was young and blond and bouncy and had a boyfriend who picked her up after school in a blue Camaro. Mrs. Trask was shaped like a Moorish pillow and did her hair in braids and laughed boomingly. And there was Miss Bird.

Charles had known he would end up with Miss Bird. He had *known* that. It had been inevitable. Because Miss Bird obviously wanted to destroy him. She did not allow children to go to the basement. The basement,

Miss Bird said, was where the boilers were kept, and well-groomed ladies and gentlemen would never go down *there*, because basements were nasty, sooty old things. Young ladies and gentlemen do not go to the basement, she said. They go to the *bathroom*.

Charles squirmed again.

Miss Bird cocked an eye at him. "Charles," she said clearly, still pointing her pointer at Bolivia, "do you need to go to the bathroom?"

Cathy Scott in the seat ahead of him giggled, wisely covering her mouth.

Kenny Griffen sniggered and kicked Charles under his desk. Charles went bright red.

"Speak up, Charles," Miss Bird said brightly. "Do you need to—"

(urinate she'll say urinate she always does)

"Yes, Miss Bird."

"Yes, what?"

"I have to go to the base—to the bathroom."

Miss Bird smiled. "Very well, Charles. You may go to the bathroom and urinate. Is that what you need to do? Urinate?"

Charles hung his head, convicted.

"Very well, Charles. You may do so. And next time kindly don't wait to be asked."

General giggles. Miss Bird rapped the board with her pointer.

Charles trudged up the row toward the door, thirty pairs of eyes boring into his back, and every one of those kids, including Cathy Scott, knew that he was going into the bathroom to urinate. The door was at least a football field's length away. Miss Bird did not go on with the lesson but kept her silence until he had opened the door, entered the blessedly empty hall, and shut the door again.

He walked down toward the boys' bathroom

(basement basement basement IF I WANT)

dragging his fingers along the cool tile of the wall, letting them bounce over the thumbtack-stippled bulletin board and slide lightly across the red

(BREAK GLASS IN CASE OF EMERGENCY)

fire-alarm box.

Miss Bird liked it. Miss Bird liked making him have a red face. In front of Cathy Scott—who never needed to go to the basement, was that fair?—and everybody else.

Old b-i-t-c-h, he thought. He spelled because he had decided last year God didn't say it was a sin if you spelled.

He went into the boys' bathroom.

It was very cool inside, with a faint, not unpleasant smell of chlorine hanging pungently in the air. Now, in the middle of the morning, it was clean and deserted, peaceful and quite pleasant, not at all like the smoky, stinky cubicle at the Star Theatre downtown.

The bathroom

(!basement!)

was built like an L, the short side lined with tiny square mirrors and white porcelain washbowls and a paper towel dispenser,

(NIBROC)

the longer side with two urinals and three toilet cubicles.

Charles went around the corner after glancing morosely at his thin, rather pallid face in one of the mirrors.

The tiger was lying down at the far end, just underneath the pebbly-white window. It was a large tiger, with tawny Venetian blinds and dark stripes laid across its pelt. It looked up alertly at Charles, and its green eyes narrowed. A kind of silky, purring grunt issued from its mouth. Smooth muscles flexed, and the tiger got to its feet. Its tail switched, making little chinking sounds against the porcelain side of the last urinal.

The tiger looked quite hungry and very vicious.

Charles hurried back the way he had come. The door seemed to take forever to wheeze pneumatically closed behind him, but when it did, he considered himself safe. This door only swung in, and he could not remember ever reading or hearing that tigers are smart enough to open doors.

Charles wiped the back of his hand across his nose. His heart was thumping so hard he could hear it. He still needed to go to the basement, worse than ever.

He squirmed, winced, and pressed a hand against his belly. He *really* had to go to the basement. If he could only be sure no one would come, he could use the girls'. It was right across the hall. Charles looked at it longingly, knowing he would never dare, not in a million years. What if Cathy Scott should come? Or—black horror!—what if *Miss Bird* should come?

Perhaps he had imagined the tiger.

He opened the door wide enough for one eye and peeked in.

The tiger was peeking back from around the angle of the L, its eye a sparkling green. Charles fancied he could see a tiny blue fleck in that deep brilliance, as if the tiger's eye had eaten one of his own. As if—

A hand slid around his neck.

Charles gave a stifled cry and felt his heart and stomach cram up into his throat. For one terrible moment he thought he was going to wet himself.

It was Kenny Griffen, smiling complacently. "Miss Bird sent me after you 'cause you been gone six years. You're in trouble."

"Yeah, but I can't go to the basement," Charles said, feeling faint with the fright Kenny had given him.

"Yer constipated!" Kenny chortled gleefully. "Wait'll I tell *Caaathy!*"

"You better not!" Charles said urgently. "Besides, I'm not. There's a tiger in there."

"What's he doing?" Kenny asked. "Takin' a piss?"

"I don't know," Charles said, turning his face to the wall. "I just wish he'd go away." He began to weep.

"Hey," Kenny said, bewildered and a little frightened. "Hey."

"What if I *have* to go? What if I can't help it? Miss Bird'll say—"

"Come on," Kenny said, grabbing his arm in one hand and pushing the door open with the other. "You're making it up."

They were inside before Charles, terrified, could break free and cower back against the door.

"Tiger," Kenny said disgustedly. "Boy, Miss Bird's gonna *kill* you."

"It's around the other side."

Kenny began to walk past the washbowls. "Kitty-kitty-kitty? Kitty?"

"Don't!" Charles hissed.

Kenny disappeared around the corner. "Kitty-kitty? Kitty-kitty? Kit—"

Charles darted out the door again and pressed himself against the wall, waiting, his hands over his mouth and his eyes squinched shut, waiting, waiting for the scream.

There was no scream.

He had no idea how long he stood there, frozen, his bladder bursting. He looked at the door to the boys' basement. It told him nothing. It was just a door.

He wouldn't.

He couldn't.

But at last he went in.

The washbowls and the mirrors were neat, and the faint smell of chlorine was unchanged. But there seemed to be a smell under it. A faint, unpleasant smell, like freshly sheared copper.

With groaning (but silent) trepidation, he went to the corner of the L and peeped around.

The tiger was sprawled on the floor, licking its large paws with a long pink tongue. It looked incuriously at Charles. There was a torn piece of shirt caught in one set of claws.

But his need was a white agony now, and he couldn't help it. He had to. Charles tiptoed back to the white porcelain basin closest the door.

Miss Bird slammed in just as he was zipping his pants.

"Why, you dirty, filthy little boy," she said almost reflectively.

Charles was keeping a weather eye on the corner. "I'm sorry, Miss Bird . . . the tiger . . . I'm going to clean the sink . . . I'll use soap ... I swear I will . . ."

"Where's Kenneth?" Miss Bird asked calmly.

"I don't know."

He didn't, really.

"Is he back there?"

"No!" Charles cried.

Miss Bird stalked to the place where the room bent. "Come here, Kenneth. Right this moment."

"Miss Bird—"

But Miss Bird was already around the corner. She meant to pounce. Charles thought Miss Bird was about to find out what pouncing was really all about.

He went out the door again. He got a drink at the drinking fountain. He looked at the American flag hanging over the entrance to the gym. He looked at the bulletin board. Woodsy Owl said GIVE A HOOT, DON'T POLLUTE. Officer Friendly said NEVER RIDE WITH STRANGERS. Charles read everything twice.

Then he went back to the classroom, walked down his row to his seat with his eyes on the floor, and slid into his seat. It was a quarter to eleven. He took out *Roads to Everywhere* and began to read about Bill at the Rodeo.

THE CHIMNEY
RAMSEY CAMPBELL

MAYBE MOST OF it was only fear. But not the last thing, not that. To blame my fear for that would be worst of all.

I was twelve years old and beginning to conquer my fears. I even went upstairs to do my homework, and managed to ignore the chimney. I had to be brave, because of my parents—because of my mother.

She had always been afraid for me. The very first day I had gone to school I'd seen her watching. Her expression had reminded me of the face of a girl I'd glimpsed on television, watching men lock her husband behind bars; I was frightened all that first day. And when children had hysterics or began to bully me, or the teacher lost her temper, these things only confirmed my fears—and my mother's, when I told her what had happened each day.

Now I was at grammar school. I had been there for much of a year. I'd felt awkward in my new uniform and old shoes; the building seemed enormous, crowded with too many strange children and teachers. I'd felt I was an outsider; friendly approaches made me nervous and sullen, when people laughed and I didn't know why I was sure they were laughing at me. After a while the other boys treated me as I seemed to want to be treated: the lads from the poorer districts mocked my suburban accent, the suburban boys sneered at my old shoes.

Often I'd sat praying that the teacher wouldn't ask me a question I couldn't answer, sat paralysed by my dread of having to stand up in the waiting watchful silence. If a teacher shouted at someone my heart jumped painfully; once I'd felt the stain of my shock creeping insidiously down my thigh. Yet I did well in the end-of-term examinations, because I was terrified of failing; for nights afterwards they were another reason why I couldn't sleep.

My mother read the signs of all this on my face. More and more, once I'd told her what was wrong, I had to persuade her there was nothing worse that I'd kept back. Some mornings as I lay in bed, trying to hold back half-past seven, I'd be sick; I would grope miserably downstairs, white-faced, and my mother would keep me home. Once or twice, when my fear wasn't quite enough, I made myself sick. "Look at him. You can't expect him to go like that"—but my father would only shake his head and grunt, dismissing us both.

I knew my father found me embarrassing. This year he'd had less time for me than usual; his shop— The Anything Shop, nearby in the suburbanised village—was failing to compete with the new supermarket. But before that trouble I'd often seen him staring up at my mother and me: both of us taller than him, his eyes said, yet both scared of our own shadows. At those times I glimpsed his despair.

So my parents weren't reassuring. Yet at night I tried to stay with them as long as I could—for my worst fears were upstairs, in my room.

It was a large room, two rooms knocked into one by the previous owner. It overlooked the small back gardens. The smaller of the fireplaces had been bricked up; in winter, the larger held a fire, which my mother always feared would set fire to the room—but she let it alone, for I'd screamed when I thought she was going to take that light away: even though the firelight only added to the terrors of the room.

The shadows moved things. The mesh of the fireguard fluttered enlarged on the wall; sometimes, at the edge of sleep, it became a swaying web, and its spinner came sidling down from a corner of the ceiling. Everything was unstable; walls shifted, my clothes crawled on the back of the chair. Once, when I'd left my jacket slumped over the chair, the collar's dark upturned lack of a face began to nod forward stealthily; the holes at the ends of the sleeves worked like mouths, and I didn't dare get up to hang the jacket properly. The room grew in the dark: sounds outside, footsteps and laughter, dogs encouraging each other to bark, only emphasised the size of my trap of darkness, how distant everything else was. And there was a dimmer room in the mirror of the wardrobe beyond the foot of the bed. There was a bed in that room, and beside it a dim nightlight in a plastic lantern. Once I'd awakened to see a face staring dimly at me from the mirror; a figure had sat up when I had, and I'd almost cried out. Often I'd stared at the dim staring face, until I'd had to hide beneath the sheets.

Of course this couldn't go on for the rest of my life. On my twelfth birthday I set about the conquest of my room.

I was happy amid my presents. I had a jigsaw, a box of coloured pencils, a book of space stories. They had come from my father's shop, but they were mine now. Because I was relaxed, no doubt because she wished I could always be so, my mother said "Would you be happier if you went to another school?"

It was Saturday; I wanted to forget Monday. Besides, I imagined all schools were as frightening. "No, I'm all right," I said.

"Are you happy at school now?" she said incredulously.

"Yes, it's all right."

"Are you sure?"

"Yes, really, it's all right. I mean, I'm happy now."

The snap of the letter slot saved me from further lying. Three birthday cards: two from neighbours who talked to me when I served them in the shop—an old lady who always carried a poodle, our next-door neighbour Dr. Flynn—and a card from my parents. I'd seen all three cards in the shop, which spoiled them somehow.

As I stood in the hall I heard my father. "You've got to control yourself," he was saying. "You only upset the child. If you didn't go on at him he wouldn't be half so bad."

It infuriated me to be called a child. "But I worry so," my mother said brokenly. "He can't look after himself."

"You don't let him try. You'll have him afraid to go up to bed next."

But I already was. Was that my mother's fault? I remembered her putting the nightlight by my bed when I was very young, checking the flex and the bulb each night—I'd taken to lying awake, dreading that one or the other would fail. Standing in the hall, I saw dimly that my mother and I encouraged each other's fears. One of us had to stop. I had to stop. Even when I was frightened, I mustn't let her see. It wouldn't be the first time I'd hidden my feelings from her. In the living-room I said "I'm going upstairs to play."

Sometimes in summer I didn't mind playing there—but this was March, and a dark day. Still, I could switch the light on. And my room contained the only table I could have to myself and my jigsaw.

I spilled the jigsaw onto the table. The chair sat with its back to the dark yawn of the fireplace; I moved it hastily to the foot of the bed, facing the door. I spread the jigsaw. There was a piece of the edge, another. By lunchtime I'd assembled the edge. "You look pleased with yourself," my father said.

I didn't notice the approach of night. I was fitting together my own blue sky above fragmented cottages. After dinner I hurried to put in the pieces I'd placed mentally while eating. I hesitated outside my room. I should have to reach into the dark for the light switch. When I did, the wallpaper filled with bright multiplied aeroplanes and engines. I wished we could afford to redecorate my room, it seemed childish now.

The fireplace gaped. I retrieved the fireguard from the cupboard under the stairs, where my father had stored it now the nights were a little warmer. It covered the soot-encrusted yawn. The room felt comfortable now. I'd never seen before how much space it gave me for play.

I even felt safe in bed. I switched out the nightlight—but that was too much; I grabbed the light. I didn't mind its glow on its own, without the jagged lurid jig of the shadows. And the fireguard was comforting. It made me feel that nothing could emerge from the chimney.

On Monday I took my space stories to school. People asked to look at them; eventually they lent me books. In the following weeks some of my fears began to fade. Questions darting from desk to desk still made me uneasy, but if I had to stand up without the answer at least I knew the other boys weren't sneering at me, not all of them; I was beginning to have friends. I started to sympathise with their own ignorant silences. In the July examinations I was more relaxed, and scored more marks. I was even sorry to leave my friends for the summer; I invited some of them home.

I felt triumphant. I'd calmed my mother and my room all by myself, just by realising what had to be done. I suppose that sense of triumph helped me. It must have given me a little strength with which to face the real terror.

It was early August, the week before our holiday. My mother was worrying over the luggage, my father was trying to calculate his accounts; they were beginning to chafe against each other. I went to my room, to stay out of their way.

I was halfway through a jigsaw, which one of my friends had swapped for mine. People sat in back gardens, letting the evening settle on them; between the houses the sky was pale yellow. I inserted pieces easily, relaxed by the nearness of our holiday. I listened to the slowing of the city, a radio fluttering along a street, something moving behind the fireguard, in the chimney.

No. It was my mother in the next room, moving luggage. It was someone dragging, dragging something, anything, outside. But I couldn't deceive my ears. In the chimney something large had moved.

It might have been a bird, stunned or dying, struggling feebly—except that a bird would have sounded wilder. It could have been a mouse, even a rat, if such things are found in chimneys. But it sounded like a large body, groping stealthily in the dark: something large that didn't want me to hear it. It sounded like the worst terror of my infancy.

I'd almost forgotten that. When I was three years old my mother had let me watch television; it was bad for my eyes, but just this once, near Christmas—I'd seen two children asleep in bed, an enormous crimson man emerging from the fireplace, creeping towards them. They weren't going to wake up! "Burglar! Burglar!" I'd screamed, beginning to cry. "No, dear, it's Father Christmas," my mother said, hastily switching off the television. "He always comes out of the chimney."

Perhaps if she'd said "down" rather than "out of" . . . For months after that, and in the weeks before several Christmases, I lay awake listening fearfully for movement in the chimney: I was sure a fat grinning figure would creep upon me if I slept. My mother had told me the presents that appeared at the end of my bed were left by Father Christmas, but now the mysterious visitor had a face and a huge body, squeezed into the dark chimney among the soot. When I heard the wind breathing in the chimney I had to trap my screams between my lips.

Of course at last I began to suspect there was no Father Christmas: how did he manage to steal into my father's shop for my presents? He was a childish idea, I was almost sure—but I was too embarrassed to ask my parents or my friends. But I wanted not to believe in him, that silent lurker in the chimney; and now I didn't, not really. Except that something large was moving softly behind the fireguard.

It had stopped. I stared at the wire mesh, half expecting a fat pale face to stare out of the grate. There was nothing but the fenced dark. Cats were moaning in a garden, an ice-cream van wandered brightly. After a while I forced myself to pull the fireguard away.

I was taller than the fireplace now. But I had to stoop to peer up the dark soot-ridged throat, and then it loomed over me, darkness full of menace, of the threat of a huge figure bursting out at me, its red mouth crammed with sparkling teeth. As I peered up, trembling a little, and tried to persuade myself that what I'd heard had flown away or scurried back into its hole, soot came trickling down from the dark—and I heard the sound of a huge body squeezed into the sooty passage, settling itself carefully, more comfortably in its burrow.

I slammed the guard into place and fled. I had to gulp to breathe. I ran onto the landing, trying to catch my breath so as to cry for help. Downstairs my mother was nervously asking whether she should pack another of my father's shirts. "Yes, if you like," he said irritably.

No, I mustn't cry out. I'd vowed not to upset her. But how could I go back into my room? Suddenly I had a thought that seemed to help. At school we'd learned how sweeps had used to send small boys up chimneys; there had hardly been room for the boys to climb. How could a large man fit in there?

He couldn't. Gradually I managed to persuade myself. At last I opened the door of my room. The chimney was silent; there was no wind. I tried not to think that he was holding himself still, waiting to squeeze out stealthily, waiting for the dark. Later, lying in the steady glow from my plastic lantern, I tried to hold on to the silence, tried to believe there was nothing near me to shatter it. There was nothing except, eventually, sleep.

Perhaps if I'd cried out on the landing I would have been saved from my fear. But I was happy with my rationality. Only once, nearly asleep, I wished the fire were lit, because it would burn anything that might be hiding in the chimney; that had never occurred to me before. But it didn't matter, for the next day we went on holiday.

My parents liked to sleep in the sunlight, beneath newspaper masks; in the evenings they liked to stroll along the wide sandy streets. I didn't, and befriended Nigel, the son of another family who were staying in the boarding-house. My mother encouraged the friendship: such a nice boy, two years older than me; he'd look after me. He had money, and the hope of a moustache shadowing his pimply upper lip. One evening he took me to the fairground, where we met two girls; he and the older girl went to buy ice creams while her young friend and I stared at each other timidly. I couldn't believe the young girl didn't like jigsaws. Later, while I was contradicting her, Nigel and his companion disappeared behind the Ghost Train—but Nigel reappeared almost at once, red-faced, his left cheek redder. "Where's Rose?" I asked, bewildered.

"She had to go." He seemed furious that I'd asked.

"Isn't she coming back?"

"No." He was glancing irritably about for a change of subject. "What a super bike," he said, pointing as it glided between the stalls. "Have you got a bike?"

"No," I said. "I keep asking Father Christmas, but—"

I wished that hadn't got past me, for he was staring at me, winking at the young girl. "Do you still believe in him?" he demanded scornfully.

"No, of course I don't. I was only kidding." Did he believe me? He was edging towards the young girl now, putting his arm around her; soon she excused herself, and didn't come back—I never knew her name. I was annoyed he'd made her run away. "Where did Rose go?" I said persistently.

He didn't tell me. But perhaps he resented my insistence, for as the family left the boarding-house I heard him say loudly to his mother "He still believes in Father Christmas." My mother heard that too, and glanced anxiously at me.

Well, I didn't. There was nobody in the chimney, waiting for me to come home. I didn't care that we were going home the next day. That night I pulled away the fireguard and saw a fat pale face hanging down into the fireplace, like an underbelly, upside down and smiling. But I managed to wake, and eventually the sea lulled me back to sleep.

As soon as we reached home I ran upstairs. I uncovered the fireplace and stood staring, to discover what I felt. Gradually I filled with the scorn Nigel would have felt, had he known of my fear. How could I have been so childish? The chimney was only a passage for smoke, a hole into which the wind wandered sometimes. That night, exhausted by the journey home, I slept at once.

The nights darkened into October; the darkness behind the mesh grew thicker. I'd used to feel, as summer waned, that the chimney was insinuating its darkness into my room. Now the sight only reminded me I'd have a fire soon. The fire would be comforting.

It was October when my father's Christmas cards arrived, on a Saturday; I was working in the shop. It annoyed him to have to anticipate Christmas so much, to compete with the supermarket. I hardly noticed the cards: my head felt muffled, my body cold—perhaps it was the weather's sudden hint of winter.

My mother came to the shop that afternoon. I watched her pretend not to have seen the cards. When I looked away she began to pick them up timidly, as if they were unfaithful letters, glancing anxiously at me. I didn't know what was in her mind. My head was throbbing. I wasn't going home sick; I earned pocket money in the shop. Besides, I didn't want my father to think I was still weak.

Nor did I want my mother to worry. That night I lay slumped in a chair, pretending to read. Words trickled down the page; I felt like dirty clothes someone had thrown on the chair. My father was at the shop taking stock. My mother sat gazing at me. I pretended harder; the words waltzed slowly. At last she said "Are you listening?"

I was now, though I didn't look up. "Yes," I said hoarsely, unplugging my throat with a roar.

"Do you remember when you were a baby? There was a film you saw, of Father Christmas coming out of the chimney." Her voice sounded bravely careless, falsely light, as if she were determined to make some awful revelation. I couldn't look up. "Yes," I said.

Her silence made me glance up. She looked as she had on my first day at school: full of loss, of despair. Perhaps she was realising I had to grow up, but to my throbbing head her look suggested only terror—as if she were about to deliver me up as a sacrifice. "I couldn't tell you the truth then," she said. "You were too young."

The truth was terror; her expression promised that. "Father Christmas isn't really like that," she said.

My illness must have shown by then. She gazed at me; her lips trembled. "I can't," she said, turning her face away. "Your father must tell you."

But that left me poised on the edge of terror. I felt unnerved, rustily tense. I wanted very much to lie down. "I'm going to my room," I said. I stumbled upstairs, hardly aware of doing so. As much as anything I was fleeing her unease. The stairs swayed a little, they felt unnaturally soft underfoot. I hurried dully into my room. I slapped the light switch and missed. I was walking uncontrollably forward into blinding dark. A figure came to meet me, soft and huge in the dark of my room.

I cried out. I managed to stagger back onto the landing, grabbing the light switch as I went. The lighted room was empty: My mother came running upstairs, almost falling. "What is it, what is it?" she cried.

I mustn't say. "I'm ill. I feel sick." I did, and a minute later I was. She patted my back as I knelt by the toilet. When she'd put me to bed she made to go next door for the doctor. "Don't leave me," I pleaded. The walls of the room swayed as if tugged by firelight; the fireplace was huge and very dark. As soon as my father opened the front door she ran downstairs, crying "He's ill, he's ill! Go for the doctor!"

The doctor came and prescribed for my fever. My mother sat up beside me. Eventually my father came to suggest it was time she went to bed. They were going to leave me alone in my room. "Make a fire," I pleaded.

My mother touched my forehead. "But you're burning," she said.

"No, I'm cold! I want a fire! Please!" So she made one, tired as she was. I saw my father's disgust as he watched me use her worry against her to get what I wanted, his disgust with her for letting herself be used.

I didn't care. My mother's halting words had overgrown my mind. What had she been unable to tell me? Had it to do with the sounds I'd heard in the chimney? The room lolled around me; nothing was sure. But the fire would make sure for me. Nothing in the chimney could survive it.

I made my mother stay until the fire was blazing. Suppose a huge shape burst forth from the hearth, dripping fire? When at last I let her go I lay lapped by the firelight and meshy shadows, which seemed lulling now, in my warm room.

I felt feverish, but not unpleasantly. I was content to voyage on my rocking bed; the ceiling swayed past above me. While I slept the fire went out. My fever kept me warm; I slid out of bed and, pulling away the fireguard, reached up the chimney. At the length of my arms I touched something heavy, hanging down in the dark; it yielded, then soft fat fingers groped down and closed on my wrist. My mother was holding my wrist as she washed my hands. "You mustn't get out of bed," she said when she realised I was awake.

I stared stupidly at her. "You'd got out of bed. You were sleepwalking," she explained. "You had your hands right up the chimney." I saw now that she was washing caked soot from my hands; tracks of ash led towards the bed.

It had been only a dream. One moment the fat hand had been gripping my wrist, the next it was my mother's cool slim fingers. My mother played word games and timid chess with me while I stayed in bed, that day and the next.

The third night I felt better. The fire fluttered gently; I felt comfortably warm. Tomorrow I'd get up. I should have to go back to school soon, but I didn't mind that unduly. I lay and listened to the breathing of the wind in the chimney.

When I awoke the fire had gone out. The room was full of darkness. The wind still breathed, but it seemed somehow closer. It was above me. Someone was standing over me. It couldn't be either of my parents, not in the sightless darkness.

I lay rigid. Most of all I wished that I hadn't let Nigel's imagined contempt persuade me to do without a nightlight. The breathing was slow, irregular; it sounded clogged and feeble. As I tried to inch silently towards the far side of the bed, the source of the breathing stooped towards me. I felt its breath waver on my face, and the breath sprinkled me with something like dry rain.

When I had lain paralysed for what felt like blind hours, the breathing went away. It was in the chimney, dislodging soot; it might be the wind. But I knew it had come out to let me know that whatever the fire had done to it, it hadn't been killed. It had emerged to tell me it would come for me on Christmas Eve. I began to scream.

I wouldn't tell my mother why. She washed my face, which was freckled with soot. "You've been sleepwalking again," she tried to reassure me, but I wouldn't let her leave me until daylight. When she'd gone I saw the ashy tracks leading from the chimney to the bed.

Perhaps I had been sleepwalking and dreaming. I searched vainly for my nightlight. I would have been ashamed to ask for a new one, and that helped me to feel I could do without. At dinner I felt secure enough to say I didn't know why I had screamed.

"But you must remember. You sounded so frightened. You upset me."

My father was folding the evening paper into a thick wad the size of a pocketbook, which he could read beside his plate. "Leave the boy alone," he said. "You imagine all sorts of things when you're feverish. I did when I was his age."

It was the first time he'd admitted anything like weakness to me. If he'd managed to survive his nightmares, why should mine disturb me more? Tired out by the demands of my fever, I slept soundly that night. The chimney was silent except for the flapping of flames.

But my father didn't help me again. One November afternoon I was standing behind the counter, hoping for customers. My father pottered, grumpily fingering packets of nylons, tins of pet food, Dinky toys, baby's rattles, cards, searching for signs of theft. Suddenly he snatched a Christmas card and strode to the counter. "Sit down," he said grimly.

He was waving the card at me, like evidence. I sat down on a shelf, but then a lady came into the shop; the bell thumped. I stood up to sell her nylons. When she'd gone I gazed at my father, anxious to hear the worst. "Just sit down," he said.

He couldn't stand my being taller than he was. His size embarrassed him, but he wouldn't let me see that; he pretended I had to sit down out of respect. "Your mother says she tried to tell you about Father Christmas," he said.

She must have told him that weeks earlier. He'd put off talking to me—because we'd never been close, and now we were growing further apart. "I don't know why she couldn't tell you," he said.

But he wasn't telling me either. He was looking at me as if I were a stranger he had to chat to. I felt uneasy, unsure now that I wanted to hear what he had to say. A man was approaching the shop. I stood up, hoping he'd interrupt.

He did, and I served him. Then, to delay my father's revelation, I adjusted stacks of tins. My father stared at me in disgust. "If you don't watch out you'll be as bad as your mother."

I found the idea of being like my mother strange, indefinably disturbing. But he wouldn't let me be like him, wouldn't let me near. All right, I'd be brave, I'd listen to what he had to say. But he said "Oh, it's not worth me trying to tell you. You'll find out."

He meant I must find out for myself that Father Christmas was a childish fantasy. He didn't mean he wanted the thing from the chimney to come for me, the disgust in his eyes didn't mean that, it didn't. He meant that I had to behave like a man.

And I could. I'd show him. The chimney was silent. I needn't worry until Christmas Eve. Nor then. There was nothing to come out.

One evening as I walked home I saw Dr. Flynn in his front room. He was standing before a mirror, gazing at his red fur-trimmed hooded suit; he stooped to pick up his beard. My mother told me that he was going to act Father Christmas at the children's hospital. She seemed on the whole glad that I'd seen. So was I: it proved the pretence was only for children.

Except that the glimpse reminded me how near Christmas was. As the nights closed on the days, and the days rushed by—the end-of-term party, the turkey, decorations in the house—I grew tense, trying to prepare myself. For what? For nothing, nothing at all. Well, I would know soon—for suddenly it was Christmas Eve.

I was busy all day. I washed up as my mother prepared Christmas dinner. I brought her ingredients, and hurried to buy some she'd used up. I stuck the day's cards to tapes above the mantelpiece. I carried home a tinsel tree which nobody had bought. But being busy only made the day move faster. Before I knew it the windows were full of night.

Christmas Eve. Well, it didn't worry me. I was too old for that sort of thing. The tinsel tree rustled when anyone passed it, light rolled in tinsel globes, streamers flinched back when doors opened. Swinging restlessly on tapes above the mantelpiece were half a dozen red-cheeked smiling bearded faces.

The night piled against the windows. I chattered to my mother about her shouting father, her elder sisters, the time her sisters had locked her in a cellar. My father grunted occasionally—even when I'd run out of subjects to discuss with my mother, and tried to talk to him about the shop. At least he hadn't noticed how late I was staying up. But he had. "It's about time everyone was in bed," he said with a kind of suppressed fury.

"Can I have some more coal?" My mother would never let me have a coal scuttle in the bedroom—she didn't want me going near the fire. "To put on now," I said. Surely she must say yes. "It'll be cold in the morning," I said.

"Yes, you take some. You don't want to be cold when you're looking at what Father—at your presents."

I hurried upstairs with the scuttle. Over its clatter I heard my father say "Are you still at that? Can't you let him grow up?"

I almost emptied the scuttle into the fire, which rose roaring and crackling. My father's voice was an angry mumble, seeping through the floor. When I carried the scuttle down my mother's eyes were red, my father looked furiously, determined. I'd always found their arguments frightening; I was glad to hurry to my room.

It seemed welcoming. The fire was bright within the mesh. I heard my mother come upstairs. That was comforting too: she was nearer now. I heard my father go next door—to wish the doctor Happy Christmas, I supposed. I didn't mind the reminder. There was nothing of Christmas Eve in my room, except the pillowcase waiting to be filled with presents on the floor at the foot of the bed. I pushed it aside with one foot, the better to ignore it.

I slid into bed. My father came upstairs; I heard further mumblings of argument through the bedroom wall. At last they stopped, and I tried to relax. I lay, glad of the silence.

A wind was rushing the house. It puffed down the chimney; smoke trickled through the fireguard. Now the wind was breathing brokenly. It was only the wind. It didn't bother me.

Perhaps I'd put too much coal on the fire. The room was hot; I was sweating. I felt almost feverish. The huge mesh flicked over the wall repeatedly, nervously, like a rapid net. Within the mirror the dimmer room danced.

Suddenly I was a little afraid. Not that something would come out of the chimney, that was stupid: afraid that my feeling of fever would make me delirious again. It seemed years since I'd been disturbed by the sight of the room in the mirror, but I was disturbed now. There was something wrong with that dim jerking room.

The wind breathed. Only the wind, I couldn't hear it changing. A fat billow of smoke squeezed through the mesh. The room seemed more oppressive now, and smelled of smoke. It didn't smell entirely like coal smoke, but I couldn't tell what else was burning. I didn't want to get up to find out.

I must lie still. Otherwise I'd be writhing about trying to clutch at sleep, as I had the second night of my fever, and sometimes in summer. I must sleep before the room grew too hot. I must keep my eyes shut. I mustn't be distracted by the faint trickling of soot, nor the panting of the wind, nor the shadows and orange light that snatched at my eyes through my eyelids.

I woke in darkness. The fire had gone out. No, it was still there when I opened my eyes: subdued orange crawled on embers, a few weak flames leapt repetitively. The room was moving more slowly now. The dim room in the mirror, the face peering out at me, jerked faintly, as if almost dead.

I couldn't look at that. I slid farther down the bed, dragging the pillow into my nest. I was too hot, but at least beneath the sheets I felt safe. I began to relax. Then I realised what I'd seen. The light had been dim, but I was almost sure the fireguard was standing away from the hearth.

I must have mistaken that, in the dim light. I wasn't feverish, I couldn't have sleepwalked again. There was no need for me to look, I was comfortable. But I was beginning to admit that I had better look when I heard the slithering in the chimney.

Something large was coming down. A fall of soot: I could hear the scattering pats of soot in the grate, thrown down by the harsh halting wind. But the wind was emerging from the fireplace, into the room. It was above me, panting through its obstructed throat.

I lay staring up at the mask of my sheets. I trembled from holding myself immobile. My held breath filled me painfully as lumps of rock. I had only to lie there until whatever was above me went away. It couldn't touch me.

The clogged breath bent nearer; I could hear its dry rattling. Then something began to fumble at the sheets over my face. It plucked feebly at them, trying to grasp them, as if it had hardly anything to grasp with. My own hands clutched at the sheets from within, but couldn't hold them down entirely. The sheets were being tugged from me, a fraction at a time. Soon I would be face to face with my visitor.

I was lying there with my eyes squeezed tight when it let go of the sheets and went away. My throbbing lungs had forced me to take shallow breaths; now I breathed silently open-mouthed, though that filled my mouth with fluff. The tolling of my ears subsided, and I realised the thing had not returned to the chimney. It was still in the room.

I couldn't hear its breathing; it couldn't be near me. Only that thought allowed me to look—that, and the desperate hope that I might escape, since it moved so slowly. I peeled the sheets down from my face slowly, stealthily, until my eyes were bare. My heartbeats shook me. In the sluggishly shifting light I saw a figure at the foot of the bed.

Its red costume was thickly furred with soot. It had its back to me; its breathing was muffled by the hood. What shocked me most was its size. It occurred to me, somewhere amid my engulfing terror, that burning shrivels things. The figure stood in the mirror as well, in the dim twitching room. A face peered out of the hood in the mirror, like a charred turnip carved with a rigid grin.

The stunted figure was still moving painfully. It edged round the foot of the bed and stooped to my pillowcase. I saw it draw the pillowcase up over itself and sink down. As it sank its hood fell back, and I saw the charred turnip roll about in the hood, as if there were almost nothing left to support it.

I should have had to pass the pillowcase to reach the door. I couldn't move. The room seemed enormous, and was growing darker; my parents were far away. At last I managed to drag the sheets over my face, and pulled the pillow, like muffs, around my ears.

I had lain sleeplessly for hours when I heard movement at the foot of the bed. The thing had got out of its sack again. It was coming towards me. It was tugging at the sheets, more strongly now. Before I could catch hold of the sheets I glimpsed a red fur-trimmed sleeve, and was screaming.

"Let go, will you," my father said irritably. "Good God, it's only me."

He was wearing Dr. Flynn's disguise, which flapped about him—the jacket, at least; his pyjama cuffs peeked beneath it. I stopped screaming and began to giggle hysterically. I think he would have struck me, but my mother ran in. "It's all right. All right," she reassured me, and explained to him "It's the shock."

He was making angrily for the door when she said "Oh, don't go yet, Albert. Stay while he opens his presents," and, lifting the bulging pillowcase from the floor, dumped it beside me.

I couldn't push it away, I couldn't let her see my terror. I made myself pull out my presents into the daylight, books, sweets, ballpoints; as I groped deeper I wondered whether the charred face would crumble when I touched it. Sweat pricked my hands; they shook with horror—they could, because my mother couldn't see them.

The pillowcase contained nothing but presents and a pinch of soot. When I was sure it was empty I slumped against the headboard, panting. "He's tired," my mother said, in defence of my ingratitude. "He was up very late last night."

Later I managed an accident, dropping the pillow-case on the fire downstairs. I managed to eat Christmas dinner, and to go to bed that night. I lay awake, even though I was sure nothing would come out of the chimney now. Later I realised why my father had come to my room in the morning dressed like that; he'd intended me to catch him, to cure me of the pretence. But it was many years before I enjoyed Christmas very much.

When I left school I went to work in libraries. Ten years later I married. My wife and I crossed town weekly to visit my parents. My mother chattered; my father was taciturn. I don't think he ever quite forgave me for laughing at him.

One winter night our telephone rang. I answered it, hoping it wasn't the police. My library was then suffering from robberies. All I wanted was to sit before the fire and imagine the glittering cold outside. But it was Dr. Flynn.

"Your parents' house is on fire," he told me. "Your father's trapped in there. Your mother needs you."

They'd had a friend to stay. My mother had lit the fire in the guest room, my old bedroom. A spark had eluded the fireguard; the carpet had caught fire. Impatient for the fire engine, my father had run back into the house to put the fire out, but had been overcome. All this I learned later. Now I drove coldly across town, towards the glow in the sky.

The glow was doused by the time I arrived. Smoke scrolled over the roof. But my mother had found a coal sack and was struggling still to run into the house, to beat out the fire; her friend and Dr. Flynn held her back. She dropped the sack and ran to me. "Oh, it's your father. It's Albert," she repeated through her weeping.

The firemen withdrew their hose. The ambulance stood winking. I saw the front door open, and a stretcher carried out. The path was wet and frosty. One stretcher-bearer slipped, and the contents of the stretcher spilled over the path.

I saw Dr. Flynn glance at my mother. Only the fear that she might turn caused him to act. He grabbed the sack and, running to the path, scooped up what lay scattered there. I saw the charred head roll on the lip of the sack before it dropped within. I had seen that already, years ago.

My mother came to live with us, but we could see she was pining; my parents must have loved each other, in their way. She died a year later. Perhaps I killed them both. I know that what emerged from the chimney was in some sense my father. But surely that was a premonition. Surely my fear could never have reached out to make him die that way.

SCHOOL FOR THE UNSPEAKABLE

MANLY WADE WELLMAN

BART SETWICK DROPPED off the train at Carrington and stood for a moment on the station platform, an honest-faced, well-knit lad in tweeds. This little town and its famous school would be his home for the next eight months; but which way to the school? The sun had set, and he could barely see the shop signs across Carrington's modest main street. He hesitated, and a soft voice spoke at his very elbow:

"Are you for the school?"

Startled, Bart Setwick wheeled. In the gray twilight stood another youth, smiling thinly and waiting as if for an answer. The stranger was all of nineteen years old—that meant maturity to young Setwick, who was fifteen—and his pale face had shrewd lines to it. His tall, shambling body was clad in high-necked jersey and unfashionably tight trousers. Bart Setwick skimmed him with the quick, appraising eye of young America.

"I just got here," he replied. "My name's Setwick."

"Mine's Hoag." Out came a slender hand. Setwick took it and found it froggy-cold, with a suggestion of steel-wire muscles. "Glad to meet you. I came down on the chance someone would drop off the train. Let me give you a lift to the school."

Hoag turned away, felinely light for all his ungainliness, and led his new acquaintance around the corner of the little wooden railway station. Behind the structure, half hidden in its shadow, stood a shabby buggy with a lean bay horse in the shafts.

"Get in," invited Hoag, but Bart Setwick paused for a moment. His generation was not used to such vehicles. Hoag chuckled and said, "Oh, this is only a school wrinkle. We run to funny customs. Get in."

Setwick obeyed. "How about my trunk?"

"Leave it." The taller youth swung himself in beside Setwick and took the reins. "You'll not need it tonight."

He snapped his tongue and the bay horse stirred, drew them around and off down a bush-lined side road. Its hoofbeats were oddly muffled.

They turned a corner, another, and came into open country. The lights of Carrington, newly kindled against the night, hung behind like a constellation settled down to Earth. Setwick felt a hint of chill that did not seem to fit the September evening.

"How far is the school from town?" he asked.

"Four or five miles," Hoag replied in his hushed voice. "That was deliberate on the part of the founders—they wanted to make it hard for the students to get to town for larks. It forced us to dig up our own amusements." The pale face creased in a faint smile, as if this were a pleasantry. "There's just a few of the right sort on hand tonight. By the way, what did you get sent out for?"

Setwick frowned his mystification. "Why, to go to school. Dad sent me."

"But what for? Don't you know that this is a high-class prison prep? Half of us are lunkheads that need poking along, the other half are fellows who got in scandals somewhere else. Like me." Again Hoag smiled.

Setwick began to dislike his companion. They rolled a mile or so in silence before Hoag again asked a question:

"Do you go to church, Setwick?"

The new boy was afraid to appear priggish, and made a careless show with, "Not very often."

"Can you recite anything from the Bible?" Hoag's soft voice took on an anxious tinge.

"Not that I know of."

"Good," was the almost-hearty response. "As I was saying, there's only a few of us at the school tonight—only three, to be exact. And we don't like Bible-quoters."

Setwick laughed, trying to appear sage and cynical. "Isn't Satan reputed to quote the Bible to his own—"

"What do you know about Satan?" interrupted Hoag. He turned full on Setwick, studying him with intent, dark eyes. Then, as if answering his own question: "Little enough, I'll bet. Would you like to know about him?"

"Sure I would," replied Setwick, wondering what the joke would be.

"I'll teach you after a while," Hoag promised cryptically, and silence fell again.

Half a moon was well up as they came in sight of a dark jumble of buildings.

"Here we are," announced Hoag, and then, throwing back his head, he emitted a wild, wordless howl that made Setwick almost jump out of the buggy. "That's to let the others know we're coming," he explained. "Listen!"

Back came a seeming echo of the howl, shrill, faint, and eerie. The horse wavered in its muffled trot, and Hoag clucked it back into step. They turned in at a driveway well grown up in weeds, and two minutes more brought them up to the rear of the closest building. It was dim-gray in the wash of moonbeams, with blank, inky rectangles for windows. Nowhere was there a light, but as the buggy came to a halt Setwick saw a young head pop out of a window on the lower floor.

"Here already, Hoag?" came a high, reedy voice.

"Yes," answered the youth at the reins, "and I've brought a new man with me."

Thrilling a bit to hear himself called a man, Setwick alighted. "His name's Setwick," went on Hoag. "Meet Andoff, Setwick. A great friend of mine."

Andoff flourished a hand in greeting and scrambled out over the windowsill. He was chubby and squat and even paler than Hoag, with a low forehead beneath lank, wet-looking hair, and black eyes set wide apart in a fat, stupid-looking face. His shabby jacket was too tight for him, and beneath worn knickers his legs and feet were bare. He might have been an overgrown thirteen or an undeveloped eighteen.

"Felcher ought to be along in half a second," he volunteered.

"Entertain Setwick while I put up the buggy," Hoag directed him.

Andoff nodded, and Hoag gathered the lines in his hands, but paused for a final word.

"No funny business yet, Andoff," he cautioned seriously. "Setwick, don't let this lard-bladder rag you or tell you wild stories until I come back."

Andoff laughed shrilly. "No, no wild stories," he promised. "You'll do the talking, Hoag."

The buggy trundled away, and Andoff swung his fat, grinning face to the new arrival.

"Here comes Felcher," he announced. "Felcher, meet Setwick."

Another boy had bobbed up, it seemed, from nowhere. Setwick had not seen him come around the corner of the building, or slip out of a door or window. He was probably as old as Hoag, or older, but so small as to be almost a dwarf, and frail to boot. His most notable characteristic was his hairiness. A great mop covered his head, bushed over his neck and ears, and hung unkemptly to his bright, deep-set eyes. His lips and cheeks were spread with a rank down, and a curly thatch peeped through the unbuttoned collar of his soiled white shirt. The hand he offered Setwick was almost simian in its shagginess and in the hardness of its palm. Too, it was cold and damp. Setwick remembered the same thing of Hoag's handclasp.

"We're the only ones here so far," Felcher remarked. His voice, surprisingly deep and strong for so small a creature, rang like a great bell.

"Isn't even the headmaster here?" inquired Setwick, and at that the other two began to laugh uproariously, Andoff's fife-squeal rendering an obbligato to Felcher's bell-boom. Hoag, returning, asked what the fun was.

"Setwick asks," groaned Felcher, "why the headmaster isn't here to welcome him."

More fife-laughter and bell-laughter.

"I doubt if Setwick would think the answer was funny," Hoag commented, and then chuckled softly himself.

Setwick, who had been well-brought-up, began to grow nettled.

"Tell me about it," he urged, in what he hoped was a bleak tone, "and I'll join your chorus of mirth."

Felcher and Andoff gazed at him with eyes strangely eager and yearning. Then they faced Hoag.

"Let's tell him," they both said at once, but Hoag shook his head.

"Not yet. One thing at a time. Let's have the song first."

They began to sing. The first verse of their offering was obscene, with no pretense of humor to redeem it. Setwick had never been squeamish, but he found himself definitely repelled. The second verse seemed less objectionable, but it hardly made sense:

All they tried to teach here
Now goes untaught.
Ready, steady, each here,
Knowledge we sought.
What they called disaster
Killed us not, O master!
Rule us, we beseech here,
Eye, hand, and thought.

It was something like a hymn, Setwick decided; but before what altar would such hymns be sung? Hoag must have read that question in his mind.

"You mentioned Satan in the buggy on the way out," he recalled, his knowing face hanging like a mask in the half-dimness close to Setwick. "Well, that was a Satanist song."

"It was? Who made it?"

"I did," Hoag informed him. "How do you like it?"

Setwick made no answer. He tried to sense mockery in Hoag's voice, but could not find it. "What," he asked finally, "does all this Satanist singing have to do with the headmaster?"

"A lot," came back Felcher deeply, and "A lot," squealed Andoff.

Hoag gazed from one of his friends to the others, and for the first time he smiled broadly. It gave him a toothy look.

"I believe," he ventured quietly but weightily, "that we might as well let Setwick in on the secret of our little circle."

Here it would begin, the new boy decided—the school hazing of which he had heard and read so much. He had anticipated such things with something of excitement, even eagerness, but now he wanted none of them. He did not like his three companions, and he did not like the way they approached whatever it was they intended to do. He moved backward a pace or two, as if to retreat.

Swift as darting birds, Hoag and Andoff closed in at either elbow. Their chill hands clutched him and suddenly he felt light-headed and sick. Things that had been clear in the moonlight went hazy and distorted.

"Come on and sit down, Setwick," invited Hoag, as though from a great distance. His voice did not grow loud or harsh, but it embodied real menace. "Sit on that windowsill. Or would you like us to carry you?"

At the moment Setwick wanted only to be free of their touch, and so he walked unresistingly to the sill and scrambled up on it. Behind him was the blackness of an unknown chamber, and at his knees gathered the three who seemed so eager to tell him their private joke.

"The headmaster was a proper churchgoer," began Hoag, as though he were the spokesman for the group. "He didn't have any use for devils or devil-worship.

Went on record against them when he addressed us in chapel. That was what started us."

"Right," nodded Andoff, turning up his fat, larval face. "Anything he outlawed, we wanted to do. Isn't that logic?"

"Logic and reason," wound up Felcher. His hairy right hand twiddled on the sill near Setwick's thigh. In the moonlight it looked like a big, nervous spider.

Hoag resumed. "I don't know of any prohibition of his that was easier or more fun to break."

Setwick found that his mouth had gone dry. His tongue could barely moisten his lips. "You mean," he said, "that you began to worship devils?"

Hoag nodded happily, like a teacher at an apt pupil. "One vacation I got a book on the cult. The three of us studied it, then began ceremonies. We learned the charms and spells, forward and backward—"

"They're twice as good backward," put in Felcher, and Andoff giggled.

"Have you any idea, Setwick," Hoag almost cooed, "what it was that appeared in our study the first time we burned wine and sulfur, with the proper words spoken over them?"

Setwick did not want to know. He clenched his teeth. "If you're trying to scare me," he managed to growl out, "it certainly isn't going to work."

All three laughed once more, and began to chatter out their protestations of good faith.

"I swear that we're telling the truth, Setwick," Hoag assured him. "Do you want to hear it, or don't you?"

Setwick had very little choice in the matter, and he realized it. "Oh, go ahead," he capitulated, wondering how it would do to crawl backward from the sill into the darkness of the room.

Hoag leaned toward him, with the air as of one confiding. "The headmaster caught us. Caught us red-handed."

"Book open, fire burning," chanted Felcher.

"He had something very fine to say about the vengeance of Heaven," Hoag went on. "We got to laughing at him. He worked up a frenzy. Finally he tried to take Heaven's vengeance into his own hands—tried to visit it on us, in a very primitive way. But it didn't work."

Andoff was laughing immoderately, his fat arms across his bent belly.

"He thought it worked," he supplemented between high gurgles, "but it didn't."

"Nobody could kill us," Felcher added. "Not after the oaths we'd taken, and the promises that had been made us."

"What promises?" demanded Setwick, who was struggling hard not to believe. "Who made you any promises?"

"Those we worshipped," Felcher told him. If he was simulating earnestness, it was a supreme bit of acting. Setwick, realizing this, was more daunted than he cared to show.

"When did all these things happen?" was his next question. "When?" echoed Hoag. "Oh, years and years ago."

"Years and years ago," repeated Andoff.

"Long before you were born," Felcher assured him.

They were standing close together, their backs to the moon that shone in Setwick's face. He could not see their expressions clearly. But their three voices—Hoag's soft, Felcher's deep and vibrant, Andoff's high and squeaky—were absolutely serious.

"I know what you're arguing within yourself," Hoag announced somewhat smugly. "How can we, who talk about those many past years, seem so young? That calls for an explanation, I'll admit." He paused, as if choosing words. "Time—for us—stands still. It came to a halt on that very night, Setwick; the night our headmaster tried to put an end to our worship."

"And to us," smirked the gross-bodied Andoff, with his usual air of self-congratulation at capping one of Hoag's statements.

"The worship goes on," pronounced Felcher, in the same chanting manner that he had affected once before. "The worship goes on, and we go on, too."

"Which brings us to the point," Hoag came in briskly. "Do you want to throw in with us, Setwick—make the fourth of this lively little party?"

"No, I don't," snapped Setwick vehemently.

They fell silent, and gave back a little—a trio of bizarre silhouettes against the pale moonglow. Setwick could see the flash of their staring eyes among the shadows of their faces. He knew that he was afraid, but hid his fear. Pluckily he dropped from the sill to the ground. Dew from the grass spattered his sock-clad ankles between oxfords and trouser-cuffs.

"I guess it's my turn to talk," he told them levelly. "I'll make it short. I don't like you, nor anything you've said. And I'm getting out of here."

"We won't let you," said Hoag, hushed but emphatic.

"We won't let you," murmured Andoff and Felcher together, as though they had rehearsed it a thousand times.

Setwick clenched his fists. His father had taught him to box. He took a quick, smooth stride toward Hoag and hit him hard in the face. Next moment all three had flung themselves upon him. They did not seem to strike or grapple or tug, but he went down under their assault. The shoulders of his tweed coat wallowed in sand, and he smelled crushed weeds. Hoag, on top of him, pinioned his arms with a knee on each bicep. Felcher and Andoff were stooping close.

Glaring up in helpless rage, Setwick knew once and for all that this was no schoolboy prank. Never did practical jokers gather around their victim with such staring, green-gleaming eyes, such drawn jowls, such quivering lips.

Hoag bared white fangs. His pointed tongue quested once over them.

"Knife!" he muttered, and Felcher fumbled in a pocket, then passed him something that sparkled in the moonlight.

Hoag's lean hand reached for it, then whipped back. Hoag had lifted his eyes to something beyond the huddle. He choked and whimpered inarticulately, sprang up from Setwick's laboring chest, and fell back in awkward haste. The others followed his shocked stare, then as suddenly cowered and retreated in turn.

"It's the Master!" wailed Andoff.

"Yes," roared a gruff new voice. "Your old headmaster—and I've come back to master you!"

Rising upon one elbow, the prostrate Setwick saw what they had seen—a tall, thick-bodied figure in a long dark coat, topped with a square, distorted face and a tousle of white locks. Its eyes glittered with their own pale, hard light. As it advanced slowly and heavily it emitted a snigger of murderous joy. Even at first glance Setwick was aware that it cast no shadow.

"I am in time," mouthed the newcomer. "You were going to kill this poor boy."

Hoag had recovered and made a stand. "Kill him?" he quavered, seeming to fawn before the threatening presence. "No. We'd have given him life—"

"You call it life?" trumpeted the long-coated one. "You'd have sucked out his blood to teem your own dead veins, damned him to your filthy condition. But I'm here to prevent you!"

A finger pointed, huge and knuckly, and then came a torrent of language. To the nerve-stunned Setwick it sounded like a bit from the New Testament, or perhaps from the Book of Common Prayer. All at once he remembered Hoag's avowed dislike for such quotations.

His three erstwhile assailants reeled as if before a high wind that chilled or scorched. "No, no! Don't!" they begged wretchedly.

The square old face gaped open and spewed merciless laughter. The knuckly finger traced a cross in the air, and the trio wailed in chorus as though the sign had been drawn upon their flesh with a tongue of flame.

Hoag dropped to his knees. "Don't!" he sobbed.

"I have power," mocked their tormenter. "During years shut up I won it, and now I'll use it." Again a triumphant burst of mirth. "I know you're damned and can't be killed, but you can be tortured! I'll make you crawl like worms before I'm done with you!"

Setwick gained his shaky feet. The long coat and the blocky head leaned toward him.

"Run, you!" dinned a rough roar in his ears. "Get out of here—and thank God for the chance!"

Setwick ran, staggering. He blundered through the weeds of the driveway, gained the road beyond. In the distance gleamed the lights of Carrington. As he turned his face toward them and quickened his pace he began to weep, chokingly, hysterically, exhaustingly.

He did not stop running until he reached the platform in front of the station. A clock across the street struck ten, in a deep voice not unlike Felcher's. Setwick breathed deeply, fished out his handkerchief and mopped his face. His hand was quivering like a grass stalk in a breeze.

"Beg pardon!" came a cheery hail. "You must be Setwick."

As once before on this same platform, he whirled around with startled speed. Within touch of him stood a broad-shouldered man of thirty or so, with horn-rimmed spectacles. He wore a neat Norfolk jacket and flannels. A short briar pipe was clamped in a good-humored mouth.

"I'm Collins, one of the masters at the school," he introduced himself. "If you're Setwick, you've had us worried. We expected you on that seven o'clock train, you know. I dropped down to see if I couldn't trace you."

Setwick found a little of his lost wind. "But I've—been to the school," he mumbled protestingly. His hand, still trembling, gestured vaguely along the way he had come.

Collins threw back his head and laughed, then apologized.

"Sorry," he said. "It's no joke if you really had all that walk for nothing. Why, that old place is deserted—used to be a catch-all for incorrigible rich boys. They closed it about fifty years ago, when the headmaster went mad and killed three of his pupils. As a matter of coincidence, the master himself died just this afternoon, in the state hospital for the insane."

GRANNY'S GRINNING
ROBERT SHEARMAN

SARAH DIDN'T WANT the zombie, and she didn't
know anyone else who did. Apart from Graham,
of course, but he was only four, he wanted *everything*;
his Christmas list to Santa had run to so many sheets
of paper that Daddy had said that Santa would need to
take out a second mortgage on his igloo to get that lot,
and everyone had laughed, even though Graham didn't
know what an igloo was, and Sarah was pretty sure that
Santa didn't live in an igloo anyway. Sarah had tried
to point out to her little brother why the zombies were
rubbish. "Look," she said, showing him the picture in
the catalog, "there's nothing to a zombie. They're just
the same as us. Except the skin is a bit greener, maybe.
And the eyes have whitened a bit." But Graham said that

zombies were cool because zombies ate people when they were hungry, and when Sarah scoffed Graham burst into tears like always, and Mummy told Sarah to leave Graham alone, he was allowed to like zombies if he wanted to. Sarah thought that if it was all about eating people, she'd rather have the vampire: they sucked your blood for a start, which was so much neater somehow than just chomping down on someone's flesh—and Sharon Weekes said that she'd tried out a friend's vampire, and it was great, it wasn't just the obvious stuff like the teeth growing, but your lips swelled up, they got redder and richer and plump, and if you closed your eyes and rubbed them together it felt just the same as if a boy were kissing you. As if Sharon Weekes would know, Sharon Weekes was covered in spots, and no boy had ever kissed her, if you even so much as touched Sharon her face would explode—but you know, whatever, the rubbing lips thing still sounded great. Sarah hadn't written down on her Christmas list like Graham had done, she'd simply told Santa that she'd like the vampire, please. Just the vampire, not the mummy, or the werewolf, or the demon. And definitely not the zombie.

Even before Granny had decided to stay, Sarah knew that this Christmas was going to be different. Mummy and Daddy said that if she and Graham wanted such expensive toys, then they'd have to put up with just one present this year. Once upon a time they'd have had tons of presents, and the carpet beneath the Christmas tree would have been strewn with brightly wrapped parcels of different shapes and sizes, it'd have taken hours to open the lot. But that was before Daddy left his job because he wanted to "go it alone," before the credit crunch, before those late-night arguments in the kitchen that Sarah wasn't supposed to hear. Graham groused a little about only getting one present, but Daddy said something about a second mortgage, and this time he didn't mention igloos, and this time nobody laughed. Usually the kitchen arguments were about money, but one night they were about Granny, and Sarah actually bothered to listen. "I thought she was staying with Sonia!" said Mummy. Sonia was Daddy's sister, and she had a sad smile, and ever since Uncle Jim had left her for someone less ugly she had lived alone. "She says she's fallen out with Sonia," said Daddy, "she's coming to spend Christmas with us instead." "Oh, for goodness's sakes, *for goodness's sakes*," said Mummy, and there was a banging of drawers. "Come on," said Daddy, "she's my Mummy, what was I supposed to say?" And then he added, "It might even work in our favor," and Mummy had said it better well should, and then Sarah couldn't hear any more, perhaps because they'd shut the kitchen door, perhaps because Mummy was crying again.

Most Christmases they'd spend on their own, just Sarah with Mummy and Daddy and Graham. And on Boxing Day they'd get into the car and drive down the motorway to see Granny and Granddad. Granny looked a little like Daddy, but older and slightly more feminine. And Granddad smelled of cigarettes even though he'd given up before Sarah was born. Granny and Granddad would give out presents, and Sarah and Graham would say thank you no matter what they got. And they'd have another Christmas meal, just like the day before, except this time the turkey would be drier, and there'd be Brussels sprouts rather than sausages. There wouldn't be a Boxing Day like that again. Partly because on the way home last year Mummy had said she could never spend another Christmas like that, and it had taken all of Daddy's best efforts to calm her down in the Little Chef—but mostly, Sarah supposed, because Granddad was dead. That was bound to make a difference. They'd all been to the funeral, Sarah hadn't even missed school because it was during the summer holidays, and Graham had made a nuisance of himself during the service asking if Granddad was a ghost now and going to come back from the grave. And during the whole thing Granny had sat there on the pew, all by herself, she didn't want anyone sitting next to her, not even Aunt Sonia, and Aunt Sonia was her favorite. And she'd cried, tears were streaming down her face, and Sarah had never seen Granny like that before, her face was always set fast like granite, and now with all the tears it had become soft and fat and pulpy and just a little frightening.

Four days before Christmas Daddy brought home a tree. "One of Santa's elves coming through!" he laughed, as he lugged it into the sitting room. It was enormous, and Graham and Sarah loved it, its upper branches scraped against the ceiling, they couldn't have put the fairy on the top like usual, she'd have broken her spine. Graham and Sarah began to cover it with balls and tinsel and electric lights, and Mummy said, "How much did that cost? I thought the point was to be a bit more economical this year," and Daddy said he knew what he was doing, he knew how to play the situation. They were going to give Granny the best Christmas she'd ever had! And he asked everyone to listen carefully, and then told them that this was a very important Christmas, it was the first Granny would have without Granddad. And she was likely to be a bit sad, and maybe a bit grumpy, but they'd all have to make allowances. It was to be *her* Christmas this year, whatever she wanted, it was all about making Granny happy, Granny would get the biggest slice of turkey, Granny got to choose which James Bond film to watch in the afternoon, the one on BBC1 or the one on ITV.

Could he count on Graham and Sarah for that? Could he count on them to play along? And they both said yes, and Daddy was so pleased, they were so good he'd put their presents under the tree right away. He fetched two parcels, the same size, the same shape, flat boxes, one wrapped in blue paper and the other in pink. "Now, no peeking until the big day!" he laughed, but Graham couldn't help it, he kept turning his present over and over, and shaking it, and wondering what was inside, was it a demon, was it a zombie? And Sarah had to get on with decorating the tree all by herself, but that was all right, Graham hadn't been much use, she did a better job with him out of the way.

And that was just the start of the work! The next few days were frantic! Mummy insisted that Granny come into a house as spotless and tidy as could be, that this time she wouldn't be able to find a thing wrong with it. And she made Sarah and Graham clean even the rooms that Granny wouldn't be seeing in the first place! It was all for Granny, that's what they were told, all for Granny—and if Graham sulked about that (and he did a little), Daddy said that one day someone close to *him* would die, and then *he* could have a special Christmas where everyone would run around after *him*, and Graham cheered up at that. On Christmas Eve Daddy said he was very proud of his children, and that he had a treat for them both. Early the next morning he'd be picking Granny up from her home in the country—it was a four-and-a-half-hour journey there and back, and that they'd been *so* good they were allowed to come along for the trip! Graham got very excited, and shouted a lot. And Mummy said that it was okay to take Graham, but she needed Sarah at home, there was still work for Sarah to do. And Sarah wasn't stupid, the idea of a long drive to Granny's didn't sound much like fun to her, but it had been offered as a treat, and it hurt her to be denied a treat. Daddy glared at Mummy, and Mummy glared right back, and for a thrilling moment Sarah thought they might have an argument—but they only *ever* did that in the kitchen, they still believed the kids didn't know—and then Daddy relaxed, and then laughed, and ruffled Graham's hair, and said it'd be a treat for the boys then, just the boys, and laughed once more. So that was all right.

First thing Christmas morning, still hours before sunrise, Daddy and Graham set off to fetch Granny. Graham was so sleepy he forgot to be excited. "Goodbye then!" said Daddy cheerily; "Goodbye," said Mummy, and then suddenly pulled him into a tight hug. "It'll all be all right," said Daddy. "Of course it will," said Mummy, "off you go!" She waved them off, and then turned to Sarah, who was waving along beside her.

Mummy said, "We've only got a few hours to make everything perfect," and Sarah nodded, and went to the cupboard for the vacuum cleaner. "No, no," said Mummy, "to make *you* perfect. My perfect little girl." And Mummy took Sarah by the hand, and smiled at her kindly, and led her to her own bedroom. "We're going to make you such a pretty girl," said Mummy, "they'll all see how pretty you can be. You'll like that, won't you? You can wear your nice dress. You'd like your new dress. Won't you?" Sarah didn't like her new dress, it was hard to romp about playing a vampire in it, it was hard to play at *anything* in it, but Mummy was insistent. "And we'll give you some nice jewelry," she said. "This is a necklace of mine. It's pretty. It's gold. Do you like it? My Mummy gave it to me. Just as I'm now giving it to you. Do you remember my Mummy? Do you remember the Other Granny?" Sarah didn't, but said that she did, and Mummy smiled. "She had some earrings too, shall we try you out with those? Shall we see what that's like?" And the earrings were much heavier than the plain studs Sarah was used to, they stretched her lobes out like chewing gum, they seemed to Sarah to stretch out her entire face. "Isn't that pretty?" said Mummy, and when Sarah said they hurt a bit, Mummy said she'd get used to it. Then Mummy took Sarah by the chin, and gave her a dab of lipstick—and Sarah never wore makeup, not like the girls who sat on the back row of the school bus, not even like Sharon Weekes, Mummy had always said it made them cheap. Sarah reminded her of this, and Mummy didn't reply, and so Sarah then asked if this was all for Granny, and Mummy said, "Yes, it's all for Granny," and then corrected herself, "it's for *all* of them, let's remind them what a pretty girl you are, what a pretty woman you could grow up to be. Always remember that you could have been a pretty woman." And then she wanted to give Sarah some nail varnish, nothing too much, nothing too red, just something clear and sparkling. But Sarah had had enough, she looked in the mirror and she didn't recognize the person looking back at her, she looked so much older, and greasy, and plastic, she looked just like Mummy. And tears were in her eyes, and she looked behind her reflection at Mummy's reflection, and there were tears in Mummy's eyes too—and Mummy said she was sorry, and took off the earrings, and wiped away the lipstick with a tissue. "I'm sorry," she said again, and said that Sarah needn't dress up if she didn't want to, it was her Christmas too, not just Granny's. And Sarah felt bad, and although she didn't much like the necklace she asked if she could keep it on, she lied and said it made her look pretty—and Mummy beamed a smile so wide, and gave her a hug, and said of course she could wear the necklace, anything for her darling, anything she wanted.

The first thing Granny said was, "I haven't brought you any presents, so don't expect any." "Come on in," said Daddy, laughing, "and make yourself at home!" and Granny sniffed as if she found that prospect particularly unappealing. "Hello, Mrs. Forbes," said Mummy. "Hello, Granny," said Sarah, and she felt the most extraordinary urge to curtsey. Graham trailed behind, unusually quiet, obviously quelled by a greater force than his own. "Can I get you some tea, Mrs. Forbes?" said Mummy. "We've got you all sorts, Earl Grey, Lapsang Souchong, Ceylon . . ." "I'd like some tea, not an interrogation," said Granny. She went into the lounge, and when she sat down in Daddy's armchair she sent all the scatter cushions tumbling, she didn't notice how carefully they'd been arranged and plumped. "Do you like the tree, Mummy?" Daddy asked, and Granny studied it briefly, and said it was too big, and she hoped he'd bought it on discount. Daddy started to say something about how the tree was just to keep the children happy, as if it were really their fault, but then Mummy arrived with the tea; Granny took her cup, sipped at it, and winced. "Would you like your presents, Mummy? We've got you presents." And at the mention of presents, Graham perked up: "Presents!" he said, "presents!" "Not your presents yet, old chap," laughed Daddy amiably, "Granny first, remember?" And Granny sighed and said she had no interest in presents, she could see nothing to celebrate—but she didn't want to spoil anyone else's fun, obviously, and so if they had presents to give her now would be as good a time to put up with them as any. Daddy had bought a few gifts, and labeled a couple from Sarah and Graham. It turned out that they'd bought Granny some perfume, "your favorite, isn't it?" asked Daddy, and "with their very own pocket money too!" "What use have I got in perfume now that Arthur's dead?" said Granny curtly. And tilted her face forward so that Sarah and Graham could kiss it, by way of a thank you.

Graham was delighted with his werewolf suit. "Werewolf!" he shouted, and waving the box above his head tore around the sitting room in excitement. "And if you settle down, old chap," laughed Daddy, "you can try it on for size!" They took the cellophane off the box, removed the lid, and took out the instructions for use. The recommended age was ten and above, but as Daddy said, it was just a recommendation, and besides, there were plenty of adults there to supervise. There was a furry werewolf mask, furry werewolf slippers, and an entire furry werewolf bodysuit. Granny looked disapproving. "In my day, little boys didn't want to be werewolves," she said. "They wanted to be soldiers and train drivers." Graham put the mask over his face, and almost immediately they could all see how the fur seemed to grow in response—not only outward, what would be the fun in that, but inward too, each tiny hair follicle burying itself deep within Graham's face, so you could really believe that all this fur had naturally come out of a little boy. With a crack the jaw elongated too, into something like a snout—it wasn't a full wolf's snout, of course not, this was only a toy, and you could see that the red raw gums inside that slavering mouth were a bit too rubbery to be real, but it was still effective enough for Granny to be impressed. "Goodness," she said. But that was nothing. When Daddy fastened the buckle around the suit, straight away Graham's entire body contorted in a manner that could only be described as feral. The spine snapped and popped as Graham grew bigger, and then it twisted and curved over, as if in protest that a creature on four legs should be supporting itself on two—the now-warped spine bulged angrily under the fur. Graham gave a yelp. "Doesn't that hurt?" said Mummy, and Daddy said no, these toys were all the rage, all the kids loved them. Graham tried out his new body. He threw himself around the room, snarling in almost pantomime fashion, he got so carried away whipping his tail about he nearly knocked over the coffee table—and it didn't matter, everyone was laughing at the fun, even Sarah, even Granny. "He's a proper little beast, isn't he!" Granny said. "And you see, it's also educational," Daddy leapt in, "because Graham will learn so much more about animals this way, I bet this sends him straight to the library." Mummy said, "I wonder if he'll howl at the moon!" and Daddy said, "well, of course he'll howl at the moon," and Granny said, "all wolves howl at the moon, even I know that," and Mummy looked crestfallen. "Silly Mummy," growled Graham.

From the first rip of the pink wrapping paper Sarah could see that she hadn't been given a vampire suit. But she hoped it wasn't a zombie, even when she could see the sickly green of the mask, the bloated liver spots, the word ZOMBIE! far too proudly emblazoned upon the box. She thought it must be a mistake. And was about to say something, but when she looked up at her parents she saw they were beaming at her, encouraging, urging her on, urging her to open the lid, urging her to become one of the walking dead. So she smiled back, and she remembered not to make a fuss, that it was Granny's day—and hoped they'd kept the receipt so she could swap it for a vampire later. Daddy asked if he could give her a hand, and Sarah said she could manage, but he was helping her already, he'd already got out the zombie mask, he was already enveloping her whole face within it. He helped her with the zombie slippers, thick slabs of feet with overgrown toenails and peeling skin. He helped her with the suit, snapped the buckle. Sarah felt cold all around her, as if she'd just been dipped into a

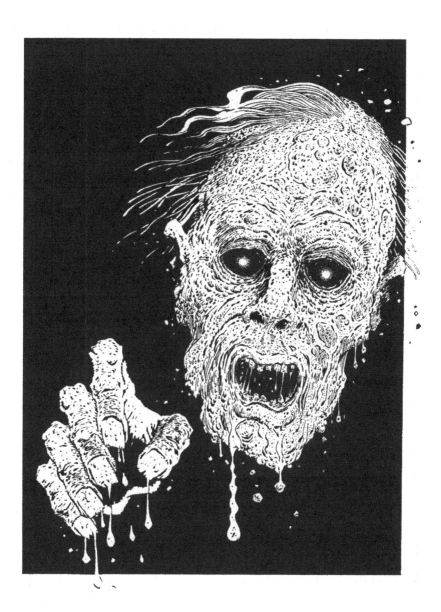

swimming pool—but it was dry inside this pool, as dry as dust, and the cold dry dust was inside her. And the surprise of it made her want to retch, but she caught herself, she swallowed it down, though there was no saliva in that swallow. Her face slumped, and bulged out a bit, like a huge spot just ready to be burst—and she felt heavier, like a sack, sodden—but sodden with what, there was no water, was there, no wetness at all, so what could she be sodden with? "Turn around!" said Daddy, and laughed, and she heard him with dead ears, and so she turned around, she lurched, the feet wouldn't let her walk properly, the body felt weighed down in all the wrong areas. Daddy laughed again, they all laughed at that, and Sarah tried to laugh too. She stuck out her arms in comic zombie fashion. "Grr," she said. Daddy's face was shining, Mummy looked just a little afraid. Granny was staring, she couldn't take her eyes off her. "Incredible," she breathed. And then she smiled, no, it wasn't a smile, she *grinned.* "Incredible." Graham had got bored watching, and had gone back to doing whatever it was that werewolves do around Christmas trees.

"And after all that excitement, roast turkey, with all the trimmings!" said Mummy. Sarah's stomach growled, though she hadn't known she was hungry. "Come on, children, toys away." "I think Sarah should wear her suit to dinner," said Granny. "I agree," said Daddy, "she's only just put it on." "All right," said Mummy. "Have it your own way. But not you, Graham. I don't want a werewolf at the dining table. I want my little boy." "That's not fair!" screamed Graham. "But werewolves don't have good table manners, darling," said Mummy. "You'll get turkey everywhere." So Graham began to cry, and it came out as a particularly plaintive howl, and he wouldn't take his werewolf off, he *wouldn't*, he wanted to live in his werewolf forever, and Mummy gave him a slap, just a little one, and it only made him howl all the more. "For God's sake, does it matter?" said Daddy, "let him be a werewolf if he wants to." "Fine," said Mummy, "they can be monsters then, let's *all* be monsters!" And then she smiled to show everyone she was happy really, she only sounded angry, really she was happy. Mummy scraped Graham's Christmas dinner into a bowl, and set it on to the floor. "Try and be careful, darling," she said, "remember how hard we worked to get this carpet clean? You'll sit at the table, won't you, Sarah? I don't know much about zombies, do zombies eat at the table?" "Sarah's sitting next to me," said Granny, and she grinned again, and her whole face lit up, she really had quite a nice face after all. And everyone cheered up at that, and it was a happy dinner, even though Granny didn't think the turkey was the best cut, and that the vegetables had been overcooked. Sarah coated her turkey with gravy, and with cranberry sauce, she even crushed then smeared peas into it just to give the meat a bit more juice—it was light and buttery, she knew, it looked so good on the fork, but no sooner had it passed her lips than the food seemed stale and ashen. "Would you pull my cracker, Sarah?" asked Granny brightly, and Sarah didn't want to, it was hard enough to grip the cutlery with those flaking hands. "Come on, Sarah," laughed Daddy, and so Sarah put down her knife and fork, and fumbled for the end of Granny's cracker, and hoped that when she pulled nothing terrible would happen—she'd got it into her head that her arm was hanging by a thread, just one firm yank and it'd come off. But it didn't—*bang!* went the cracker, Granny had won, she liked that, and she read out the joke, and everyone said they found it funny, and she even put on her paper hat. "I feel like the belle of the ball!" she said. "Dear me, I *am* enjoying myself!"

After dinner Granny and Sarah settled down on the sofa to watch the James Bond movie on TV. Mummy said she'd do the washing up, and as she needed to clean the carpet too, she might be quite a while. And Daddy volunteered to help her, he said he'd seen this Bond already. Graham wanted to pee, so they'd let him out into the garden. So it was just Granny and Sarah sitting there, just the two of them, together. "I miss Arthur," Granny said during the title sequence. "Sonia tells me I need to get over it, but what does Sonia know about love?" Sarah had nothing to say to that. Sitting on the sofa was hard for her, she was top heavy and lolled to one side. She found though that she was able to reach for the buckle on her suit. She played with it, but her fingers were too thick, she couldn't get purchase. The first time Bond kissed a woman Granny reached for Sarah's hand. Sarah couldn't be sure whether it was Granny's hand or her own that felt so leathery. "Do you know how I met Arthur?" asked Granny. Sitting in her slumped position, Sarah could feel something metal jab into her, and realized it must be the necklace that Mummy had given her. It was buried somewhere underneath all this dead male flesh. "Arthur was already married. Did you know that? Does it shock you? But I just looked at him, and said to myself, I'm having that." And there was a funny smell too, thought Sarah, and she supposed that probably *was* her. James Bond got himself into some scrapes, and then got out of them again using quips and extreme violence. Granny hadn't let go of Sarah's hand. "You know what love is? It's being prepared to let go of who you are. To change yourself entirely. Just for someone else's pleasure." The necklace was really rather sharp, but Sarah didn't mind, it felt *real*, and she tried to shift her body so it would cut into her all the more. Perhaps it would cut through the layers of skin on top of it, perhaps it would come poking out, and show that Sarah was hiding underneath!

"Before I met him, Arthur was a husband. And a father. For me, he became a nothing. A nothing." With her free hand Sarah tried at the buckle again, this time there was a panic to it, she dug in her nails but only succeeded in tearing a couple off altogether. And she knew what that smell was, Sarah had thought it had been rotting, but it wasn't, it was old cigarette smoke. Daddy came in from the kitchen. "You two lovebirds getting along?" he said. And maybe even winked. James Bond made a joke, and Granny gripped Sarah's hand so tightly that she thought it'd leave an imprint for sure. "I usually get what I want," Granny breathed. Sarah stole a look out of the window. In the frosted garden Graham had clubbed down a bird, and was now playing with its body. He'd throw it up into the air and catch it between his teeth. But he looked undecided too, as if he were wondering whether eating it might be taking things too far.

Graham had tired of the werewolf suit before his bed-time. He'd undone the belt all by himself, and left the suit in a pile on the floor. "I want a vampire!" he said. "Or a zombie!" Mummy and Daddy told him that maybe he could have another monster next Christmas, or on his birthday maybe. That wasn't good enough, and it wasn't until they suggested there might be discounted monsters in the January sales that he cheered up. He could be patient, he was a big boy. After he'd gone to bed, Granny said she wanted to turn in as well—it had been such a long day. "And thank you," she said, and looked at Sarah. "It's remarkable." Daddy said that she'd now understand why he'd asked for all those photographs; to get the resemblance just right there had been lots of special modifications, it hadn't been cheap, but he hoped it was a nice present? "The best I've ever had," said Granny. "And here's a little something for both of you." And she took out a check, scribbled a few zeroes on to it, and handed it over. She hoped this might see them through the recession. "And merry Christmas!" she said gaily.

Granny got into her nightie—but not so fast that Sarah wasn't able to take a good look at the full reality of her. She didn't think Granny's skin was very much different to the one she was wearing, the same lumps and bumps and peculiar crevasses, the same scratch marks and mottled specks. Hers was just slightly fresher. And as if Granny could read Sarah's mind, she told her to be a good boy and sit at the dressing table. "Just a little touch up," she said. "Nothing effeminate about it. Just to make you a little more you." She smeared a little rouge on to the cheeks, a dash of lipstick, mascara. "Can't do much with the eyeballs," Granny mused, "but I'll never know in the dark." And the preparations weren't just for Sarah. Granny sprayed behind both her ears from her new perfume bottle. "Just for you,

darling," she said. "Your beautiful little gift." Sarah
gestured toward the door, and Granny looked puzzled,
then brightened. "Yes, you go and take a tinkle. I'll
be waiting, my sweet." But Sarah had nothing to tinkle, had she, didn't Granny realize there was no liquid
inside her, didn't she realize she was composed of dust?
Sarah lurched past the toilet, and downstairs to the sitting room where her parents were watching the repeat
of the Queen's speech. They started when she came in.
Both looked a little guilty. Sarah tried to find the words
she wanted, and then how to say them at all, her tongue
lay cold in her mouth. "Why me?" she managed finally.

Daddy said, "I loved him. He was a good man, he was
a kind man." Mummy looked away altogether. Daddy
went on, "You do see why it couldn't have been Graham,
don't you? Why it had to be you?" And had Sarah been
a werewolf like her brother, she might at that moment
have torn out their throats, or clubbed them down with
her paws. But she was a dead man, and a dead man
who'd been good and kind. So she nodded briefly, then
shuffled her way slowly back upstairs.

"Hold me," said Granny. Sarah didn't know how to,
didn't know where to put her arms or her legs. She tried
her best, but it was all such a tangle. Granny and Sarah
lay side by side for a long time in the dark. Sarah tried

to feel the necklace under her skin, but she couldn't, it had gone. That little symbol of whatever femininity she'd had was gone. She wondered if Granny was asleep. But then Granny said, "If only it were real. But it's not real. You're not real." She stroked Sarah's face. "Oh, my love," she whispered. "Oh, my poor dead love."

You're not real, Granny was still saying, and now she was crying, and Sarah thought of how Granny had looked that day at the funeral, her face all soggy and out of shape, and she felt a stab of pity for her—and that was *it*, the pity was the jolt it needed, there was something liquid in this body after all. "You're not real," Granny said. "I am real," he said, and he leaned across, and kissed her on the lips. And the lips beneath his weren't dry, they were plump, they were moist, and now he was chewing at her face, and she was chewing right back, like they wanted to eat each other, like they were so hungry they could just eat each other alive. Sharon Weekes was wrong, it was a stray thought that flashed through his mind, Sharon Weekes didn't know the half of it. This is what it's like, this is like kissing, this is like kissing a boy.

THE CHEMISTRY
OF GHOSTS
Lisa Morton

HEY, APRIL? I think I did something really bad."

When your nine-year-old brother says that, it's never good. When he *whispers* it while you're walking home from school and there's nobody else around for at least a hundred yards, it's just weird.

Normally, I would've called Matt a dweeb or mocked his whisper, but today hadn't been a normal day. Our school had been visited by police officers who were investigating a missing classmate, but not just any classmate: they were looking for Benny Salazar, also known as my brother's best friend. I knew they'd pulled Matt out of class to talk to him, but I didn't know what had been said.

"Okay, Matt. What'd you do?"

He looked around guiltily, slowed down, and then finally stopped and turned to me, although he didn't look up. "I told the police that Benny texted me last night and said he was going to sneak out and go to Broadmore College. He heard they closed one wing there because it's supposed to be haunted, and he wanted to go see for himself."

Benny was a weird kid; he totally believed in ghosts and his phone was loaded with all kinds of ghost-hunting apps, so I could see why he'd do something like that. Me, on the other hand—I may be only three years older than Matt and Benny, but I laugh at scary movies. I'm a total science nerd, especially when it comes to chemistry; I mean, I have a poster on my bedroom wall of the periodic table because I think it's just the coolest thing ever that the whole universe is made up of just ninety-eight naturally occurring kinds of atoms (and twenty more that are man-made). I like the way the table looks, with each element having a little block and a number that indicates how it's made up. My parents keep trying to talk me into something like a business degree, even though I already know I have to go into science.

In fact, I wanted to go to Broadmore someday, because one of history's greatest chemistry professors, Dr. Cole Addison, had taught there until he'd died last year—he'd had a heart attack right in the middle of teaching a class. My friend Ling, whose mom taught economics at Broadmore, had even known Dr. Addison, although Ling said she'd never met him herself. "Mom said he was scary," Ling told me.

It wasn't the first time I'd heard that. Cole Addison was a genius, but he was also supposed to be the toughest teacher *ever*. His tests were incredibly hard, he never complimented any of his students, and he had supposedly popped a vein in class yelling at some kid and keeled over dead right there. Me, I liked tough teachers and thought I could've gotten a rare "A" in Cole Addison's class. I was sorry I'd never get to find out.

If Addison had been scary in life, he was apparently even scarier dead. A week after he died, a janitor cleaning his old classroom had freaked out when "something hit me in the back of the head, but there was no one there." A few days after that, a physics teacher had been working late in her office when Cole Addison had walked through a wall and then turned into a skeleton in front of her. She was a pretty tough professor herself, but after that encounter she refused to return to that building, and so had a lot of other people. Finally the college had closed the wing until they could figure out what to do with it.

Ling also told me that her mom said the police had indeed been searching that very building earlier today for Benny. "Are you trying to tell me Benny went to Broadmore to look for ghosts?" I asked.

Matt shuffled, bit his lip, and I thought, *Uh-oh, this is BIG.* "Well, yeah, but . . ." He broke off and finally looked me in the eye. "First, you gotta promise not to tell anybody else, especially Mom and Dad."

"Fine, I promise. Just tell me."

"I . . . I snuck out last night and went with Benny. We rode our bikes over to Broadmore."

I'm sure my jaw fell, because Matt blurted out, "You promised not to tell—!"

"I won't. What happened?"

"We found the closed wing. Benny said he saw an episode of *Haunt Hunters* set there and it was really awesome, so he wanted to see for himself.

"We found an open door, and Benny went in." Matt broke off, and I realized he was crying. My sarcasm vanished and I pulled him in for a hug.

"Ahh, Matty, whatever happened, it can't be that bad . . ."

"Yes, it can," he said, his voice muffled by my jacket, "because I didn't go in. I started to, but I got this really bad feeling and I chickened out, and then I heard Benny scream, and I ran."

I held him for a second before I gently pushed him away. "But you did the right thing: you told the police you thought Benny might be in that building, and they searched it."

"But they didn't find him."

"Right . . ." I didn't get where he was going with this.

"And I know he's there. *I know it.* And maybe none of this would've happened if I hadn't chickened out."

"But the police searched the building and didn't find him."

Matt snuffled once, rubbed away his last tear, and said, "Then I will."

I grabbed his shoulder to let him know I was serious. "Matt, you are *not* going back there. If the police didn't find him there, what makes you think you will?"

"I don't know, but . . . I gotta try, April."

Matt pulled away from me and stalked off. I knew he was going to do it, and that I wouldn't be able to stop him.

And that was when I knew I'd have to go with him.

We waited that night until after our folks had checked on us and gone to bed. Matt texted me, NOW, and it was on.

I met Matt down on the front lawn. He was already on his bike, backpack on—and a baseball bat sticking out of the pack. "What's with the bat?" I whispered.

"Protection. There could be rats or something in there."

I had to hand it to my kid brother: he *hated* rats, but he was willing to face them to save his friend.

It took us ten minutes to ride our bikes through our sleeping 'hood; it was both strange and exciting to be wheeling past the dark houses, heading for a midnight adventure. We reached the Broadmore campus, rode past some dorm buildings and a football field, and finally saw the abandoned wing in front of us. I followed Matt, since he knew where the entrance was.

We reached the double doors, got off our bikes, and looked around. It was quiet; we were alone, and the building had no lights on. I nodded at the doors and asked, "In here, right?"

Matt gulped and nodded, but was too scared to talk.

"You sure you want to do this, Matt?"

"I'm sure." He gripped his baseball bat, bravely marched up the three steps to the doors, opened them, and stepped in. I followed a few seconds later.

We were standing in a long hallway, lit only by outside light spilling in through a few windows. I could barely make out the doors lining either side of the hallway.

I turned on my phone to use as a flashlight, but Matt reached into his backpack and pulled out a couple of real flashlights. As he handed one to me, he said, "Here, these are better. I made sure they have fresh batteries."

The flashlight beam was stronger and wider, so I put my phone in my pocket. The first thing I saw were some framed photos on the wall near us; most showed sports teams and players, but one was of a tall, thin man holding a big trophy of some kind. The man looked familiar, so I read the little engraved plaque beneath the photo:

DR. COLE ADDISON WINS THE BOONE SCIENCE PRIZE IN CHEMISTRY, 2002

"Whoa—it's Dr. Addison!"

Matt pushed past me. "Whatever. C'mon, we got a lot of ground to cover in here." He shouted, "*Benny!*"

I was turning away from the photo when it *moved*— nothing huge, just a small motion of Dr. Addison's head. I stared hard at it, but nothing else happened. A trick of the light, right?

But I really had seen it move.

"Any time, April!"

I gave the photo one last look before turning to follow Matt. We worked our way down the hall, opening doors as we went. The first ten opened onto offices; each office had a sign with the room number and the occupant's name. The offices were small; they didn't even have closets, no place to hide a kid. They were numbered D-1 through D-10; D-7 had the name DR. COLE ADDISON on it.

"Wow, this was his office." I was in awe. Although most of Dr. Addison's stuff had been cleared out of the room, I still felt a thrill of recognition at seeing that he had a wall chart of the periodic table that looked just like mine. There were a few books left in a bookcase, a few scattered papers, and not much more.

Just past the offices, the main hall had two restrooms, each with three stalls, and ten classrooms about the same size as what we had at our school; the classrooms were numbered D-11 through D-20. They all held about thirty student desks, a teacher's desk, chairs, a blackboard, and a small coat closet. We looked in all the closets; it was kind of spooky that some still had coats hanging in them, even though these rooms hadn't been used in at least a year.

As we went, we both called out Benny's name a lot and then listened, but the building was completely silent. "I don't think he's here, Matt," I said, as gently as I could.

Matt nodded at a double door at the end of the hallway; the sign next to the doors read D-100. "We haven't been in there yet."

On the other side of the double doors was an amphitheater classroom, one of those where the seats are in tiers, with a desk and podium at the bottom in the center. This room could easily have seated two hundred. There was a locked emergency exit at the bottom, a small storage room behind the teacher's desk, and a door at one side that gave access to the structure beneath the tiers.

But there was no Benny.

"We've done the whole wing now," I said, as we left the big classroom.

Matt sighed heavily. "Okay."

We trudged back down the hallway until we reached the doors we'd come in through. I started to reach for the knob, but Matt held back, looking around. "Did we search everything? I just keep getting this feeling like he's here."

I thought for a few seconds before saying, "How about this: tomorrow's Saturday, right? So let's come back tomorrow when we can see more. Maybe we can even get other people to help. Sound good?"

Matt reluctantly nodded.

I shivered, suddenly cold. I was so ready to be home again, in my nice, warm bed. I reached for the knob—

It wouldn't turn.

I pushed down a jolt of panic and shook the knob, thinking maybe it was just old and rusty. It was immovable.

"What's wrong?" Matt asked.

"It's locked." Now I was really banging on the door.

"But it can't be—we came in this way." Matt tried the knob for himself.

I was about to say something when I shivered again and saw my breath come out in vapory puffs. How cold *was* it in here?

My flashlight died. I hit it against my palm, but it didn't come on. "I thought you said you put fresh batteries in here," I said to Matt.

"I did." He grabbed his phone out of his pocket. "Hey, my phone's not working."

I checked mine. It didn't work, either. We were alone in an abandoned building that we couldn't get out of, where the temperature had suddenly dropped, and where the only light came in through the windows in the doors.

Except . . . it wasn't the *only* light, because something was happening in the corridor behind us. The air was filling with a blue shimmer that got brighter as we watched, paralyzed.

"April, what is that?"

I was too scared to answer.

The light started to come together in a shape—a human shape. In a few seconds we were looking at (and *through*) a tall, thin man in a suit.

It was Dr. Cole Addison.

I gasped, and blurted out, "But you're dead—!"

Beside me, Matt half-whispered, "Do you believe in ghosts *now*?"

The figure of Dr. Cole Addison floated six feet away, looking at us. Then the mouth began to move, and I heard a voice that sounded like it was coming from the end of a tunnel and wasn't quite matching up to the lip movements.

"Your friend Benny is here."

Matt jerked forward, hefting his baseball bat. "Where?"

Dr. Addison smiled, but it wasn't friendly. "If you want to know that, you have to pass my test."

"Your test . . . ?" I remembered what I'd heard about how hard Cole Addison's tests were.

I asked, "What if your test isn't fair?"

"If you fail, you will remain here, with the other one."

Matt and I looked at each other, and I could see how scared Matt was—maybe even as scared as I was.

The floating shape said, "This test covers . . . chemistry."

Chemistry! *Okay,* I thought, *you wanted to be in one of Dr. Addison's classes, so here's your chance . . .*

Matt asked, "What kind of test?"

Dr. Addison grinned, and it looked like an effect from a horror movie. "The rules are simple: you'll be given a series of clues. If you can solve them all in one hour, you'll find your friend and you may all leave. If not . . ." He didn't have to say any more; we got it.

Matt sidestepped to me and whispered, "Chemistry . . . you can do this, right?"

Truthfully, I had no idea. But at least I could try.

"Okay," I said to the figure, "give us the first clue."

Dr. Addison began to laugh. The sound increased in volume, booming through the building until Matt and I were covering our ears in pain. Dr. Addison's head grew bigger and bigger, his mouth open, and we thought it would swallow us—and then the sound abruptly stopped. The shape vanished, and all that was left was a piece of paper fluttering down to the floor where Dr. Addison had just been.

Matt darted forward first and grabbed the paper, and just then our flashlights came back on. Matt held his up over the page. "It says, 'Find the first clue in the seat of higher learning'." Matt looked up, his brow furrowed. "What does that mean?"

"'Higher learning' usually means a college, but we're already in a college, so it's something else . . ." I thought about what we'd seen that might qualify as "higher learning." "The big classroom, with the tiers of seats—the top row would be higher learning, right?"

Matt took off running toward the double doors at the far end of the hall, and I went after him. Halfway down the hall, though, when I ran past Dr. Addison's office, I stopped and thought: *if this is going to be all about chemistry, we could use a little help.* I went into the office, looked at the few old textbooks left in the bookcase, and there was one titled *Chemistry.* I pulled it down, flipped through it, and saw stuff I thought might be useful. I also saw an old pencil nub on the desk—that might be needed for notes—so I took both pencil and book with me and I ran after Matt.

When I burst through the doors, Matt was already at the middle of the top tier, looking down at something. "What is it?" I asked.

"Come up here and see for yourself."

I joined him; he was looking down at a page from a glossy magazine, showing a swimming pool, blue and cool. We both looked at the picture, perplexed. Matt started to reach for it, but hesitated. "Do you think it's safe to touch?"

"Do you mean, does it have ghost germs or something?" I picked it up and handed it to him.

Matt flipped it over, but the back showed a piece of a photo of a car, just part of an ad. We were plainly supposed to focus on the pool.

"Okay, a swimming pool," Matt said, and then happily blurted out, "water . . . wait, even I know this one: H_2O!"

"Right! You didn't totally sleep through all your science classes."

Matt jumped excitedly. "I got it: Benny's in the bathroom!"

But something bugged me; it was *too* easy. If Addison had only wanted us to get water, he could've put a cup of water there, or a picture of the ocean, or a faucet. Why a swimming pool in particular?

Because people put chemicals in their pools to keep them clean. "Chlorine!"

Matt said, "Huh?"

"I think the answer is not water, but the main chemical that goes into pools—chlorine." I flipped open the textbook.

"Where'd you get that?"

"Dr. Addison's office." I set the book down so I could flip pages with one hand and hold the flashlight with the other. "Chlorine is number 17 on the periodic table, and its symbol is Cl." I found a blank page at the front of the book and made this note:

CLUE #1: Chlorine—17—Cl

"I still think it's water," groused Matt.

"So now how do we find the next clue?"

Matt moved his flashlight around. "There's writing on the chair."

We both bent over to look. I recognized it as the same writing on the first note Dr. Addison (or his ghost) had left us. It read: *For the next clue, go to D-12.*

Matt was already running out. "This way!"

As I gathered up the book and flashlight, I called after him, "Whoa, slow down!"

"Can't," he yelled back over his shoulder, "we've got less than an hour." He rushed out of the big classroom.

He was right. Without our phones, we had no way of telling time, so we couldn't waste even a minute. I ran after him.

D-12 was one of the smaller classrooms. It only took us a few seconds to reach it; inside, it was like all the other classrooms, with desks and chairs dimly lit by streetlight coming in through the windows . . .

Windows! Could we break a window to get out? I went up and squinted at the glass, knocked a knuckle against it. The windows were sealed shut, thick, and looked to be reinforced. But even if we could get out that way, what about Benny? And, of course, there was also Dr. Addison to think about—what would a ghost do if it found out we were trying to cheat on its test?

"What's that?"

Matt's call tore me away from thinking about windows. His flashlight beam was resting on the only object to be found on the teacher's desk at the front of the room: it was tall, metal, and painted green. There was something next to it, something connected to it with a tube . . .

"Is that a mask?"

Matt was just bending over to look when the mask jumped into the air and planted itself on his face.

His scream was choked off as invisible hands kept the mask clamped onto him, but my scream filled the classroom. I tried to help him, but the same force kept me from reaching him. I could only watch as Matt squirmed, swinging the baseball bat, his eyes wide in terror above the mask . . .

Then, as suddenly as it had started, it was over; the mask fell away from his face. Matt staggered back, panting, and I was able to run up to him.

"Are you okay?"

He couldn't quite get a word out, but he nodded.

As soon as I was sure he was fine, I turned to look at the mask and the metal cylinder. I'd seen these things in television shows, whenever there was a scene in a hospital.

"It's an oxygen mask," Matt finally got out between breaths.

"Yeah, and that's an oxygen tank." I didn't even have to open the book to know about oxygen; it's one of the most common elements, an essential part of not just the air we breathe but the ground we walk on as well. Its atomic number was 8. But I didn't want to forget anything, so I opened the book to the page where I was recording clues and wrote:

CLUE #2: Oxygen—8—O

Matt watched me write, and then asked, "So what's next?"

I swung the flashlight beam around and spotted something written on the chalkboard. "That."

As we walked up to see what it said, Matt added, "I'm pretty sure that wasn't there when we came in."

"I'm pretty sure you're right."

There on the chalkboard, in Dr. Addison's writing, was, *Go out and look at the sky.*

Matt asked, "How are we supposed to go outside?"

I shrugged. "Maybe it doesn't mean 'out' like 'outside,' but 'out' into the hallway . . ."

My brother was already heading for the door. "I don't want to stay in here with that creepy mask, anyway."

I followed him out of the classroom and into the dark, empty corridor. Matt, looking around, asked, "Now what?"

I was saved from having to answer when I glanced up and saw something happening above our heads. "Uhhh . . ."

Matt followed my gaze, and we both started to back away, slowly. The air near the ceiling was swirling, forming a blacker space, almost as if it was taking on weight. I wanted to run, but I knew I couldn't, because I'd miss the next clue.

Something brighter appeared in the center of the spinning black; it grew bigger, brighter, a light-yellow shade with some darker patches.

It was the moon, full and clear. It was huge, and even beautiful; for a few seconds, I forgot to be terrified.

"Wow," Matt muttered beside me.

It almost seemed close enough to reach out and touch. It was turning slightly, and I saw features I recognized, but with more detail than I'd ever seen before.

"That is so cool," Matt said.

I was nodding when the moon faded out, the black space vanished, and we once again stood beneath a normal ceiling.

"So," Matt said, "what does the moon have to do with chemistry? Is it made mostly of one thing?"

"I don't think so . . . I don't know. The other two were kind of easy, but this one . . ."

I sat down on the floor of the hallway with my back against a wall and opened the chemistry book, aiming my flashlight down onto the pages. First I checked the index, but there was nothing for the moon. I flipped through the pages, hoping to see a picture of the moon, or of *something* that would lead me to the answer, but . . .

Maybe I wasn't good enough after all. Maybe I wasn't as good at chemistry as I thought I was, because I couldn't seem to figure this out. I was failing Cole Addison's test—

"Uhhh, April—how long is this gonna take? Because . . ."

"I know, Matt, I know."

In desperation, I opened the book to the periodic table and started looking at all the elements, trying to find connections.

Nickel, because the moon is round like a nickel? Kind of a stretch.

Sulfur, because it was yellow like the moon? Again, that didn't feel right.

One element that I didn't know much about caught my eye: selenium. *Selenium* . . . there was something about that, something I'd read once . . .

I flipped to the index again, found an entry for selenium, went to the right page—and there it was: *selenium* was derived from the ancient Greek word for "moon."

"I got it!"

Matt jumped excitedly. "What is it?"

"Selenium. It's from an old word for moon."

I added to my list:

CLUE #3: Selenium—34—Se

Matt scanned the list so far. "What do you think it means?"

"I don't know yet. I think we've got more clues to go."

The voice of Dr. Cole Addison came from behind us: "You are correct."

We whirled to see the figure floating a few feet away. "There are five total clues," it added.

I had to give my little brother a lot of credit for being so brave just then. He stepped up to that nightmare, pointed the bat at it, and said, "Give us number four *now* and stop wasting our time." He'd come a long way from the kid who was too scared to follow his best friend into a spooky building.

Dr. Addison grabbed the bat and snapped it in two like it was a twig. He dropped the splintered pieces and said, "All right. Let's go back to the Greeks again. Who is this?" He gestured with his hand, and out of nowhere a book hit the floor by our feet.

Matt bent to examine it and exclaimed, "Oh, I have this book! It's all about mythology." I joined him, and saw the volume had landed open to a drawing of a bearded, brawny man wrestling a lion. "That," Matt said, "is Hercules, the strongest man in the world."

This was another easy one. "Titanium!"

The floating figure nodded. Matt looked at me, confused, so I explained, "Titanium is the strongest metal in the world."

But Dr. Addison wasn't done yet. "You've guessed correctly, except for one thing . . ."

"What?" I asked, my stomach already clenching in dread.

"My titanium is lacking *this* . . ."

Dr. Addison reached a translucent hand up to his face, dug his fingers in, and pulled out one of his eyes. He held it down toward us, and I saw the pale pupil still watching us, tracking our movement.

Matt shrieked. I stood frozen. The shape blinked out.

It took us a few seconds to recover before Matt could ask, "What was *that* supposed to mean?"

I shook my head, but was already checking titanium in the periodic table and writing the latest clue:

CLUE #4: Titanium—22—Ti

The symbol for titanium was Ti . . . *Ti*. "Matt, what did he say exactly?"

Matt thought for a few seconds and then said, "He said, 'my titanium is lacking this,' and then he pulled out . . ."

I grinned. "His eye. Or . . . *i*!" I took the pencil and crossed out the *i* in the symbol for titanium so Clue #4 now looked like this:

CLUE #4: Titanium—22—T̶i̶

"So," Matt said, "there's one clue left. Where do we find it?"

"Uhhh . . ." I said, looking past Matt, "*there*."

Letters were forming in the air just past Matt. As we watched, Matt breathed out, "Now he can just write in the air? Why couldn't he do that before?"

I guessed, "He's getting stronger. It probably means we don't have much time left."

The writing ended, and the words hung in the air, waving slightly like seaweed in an ocean current: *Here is your final clue: find your friend in a room of silicon.*

Then they faded away.

Matt turned to me anxiously. "Silicon? What's silicon used for? Can you have a whole room of it?"

I was already flipping through the chemistry book. "I don't know . . ." In the periodic table, silicon had an atomic weight of 14. I wrote down:

CLUE #5: Silicon—14—Si (Room)

Matt squinted at the clues. "That's all of 'em, right?"
"Yep . . ."
I looked at the list, trying to find the common thread. Something occurred to me about the final clue then. "The last clue is the only one where he gave us the name of the chemical first. I think that means it's somehow different from the others."
I took the pencil and rewrote the clues in three columns:

Chlorine	*17*	*Cl*
Oxygen	*8*	*O*
Selenium	*34*	*Se*
Titanium	*22*	*Ti (or just T, without the i)*

For the last clue, I wrote:

Room: Silicon   14   Si

"How much time do you think is left?" Matt asked.

I jumped to my feet, grinning. "It doesn't matter, because I know where Benny is!" I took off running without waiting to explain or even see if Matt was following.

As I'd looked at the columns, I'd realized that with the first four clues I was supposed to look at the symbols, which (without the *i* in titanium) spelled out: Cl-O-Se-T.

Closet.

With the fifth clue, because Dr. Addison gave us the element's name first, it was different. We were supposed to look at the number: 14. A "room of silicon" was room 14, or (as the rooms were numbered in this building) classroom D-14.

We reached D-14, tore the door open, and rushed to the closet. It was a small coat closet at the rear of the room, just two walls with clothes rods, a few old rusting hangers . . .

Nothing.

"He's not here," Matt stamped in frustration. "The police would've found him if he was."

"Wait." I crouched and ran the flashlight beam around the lower part of the closet, looking for something, *anything.* I had to be right, because there was no time to be wrong, and because I knew I *was* good at chemistry.

"The hour's probably up," Matt said in defeat.

I saw it, then: part of the wall where the wood panels didn't match. I set the flashlight down and ran my fingers along the wall.

It moved.

I heard Matt's breath catch as I applied more pressure, and found that part of the wall slid to one side, revealing a small space behind it.

Small, yes—but big enough to hide Benny. He had a gag around his mouth and he was tied up, but he was awake and making anxious sounds in his throat.

Matt helped me get him out and untied. As we lowered the gag, he said, "There's a ghost in here—!"

We cut him off. "We know. Now let's go home."

We made it to the exit without anything stopping us, and this time the doors opened easily. Matt led Benny out, and both boys whooped in relief as they ran out into the night air.

I was about to join them when I sensed a presence behind me. I turned to see the ghost there, but now Dr. Addison's smile didn't look creepy.

"I passed your test," I said, in case he was going to try to go back on the deal.

Instead he nodded and said, "You'll make a fine scientist some day."

He vanished, and I knew he was gone for good; but Cole Addison—the guy who never said anything nice to *anyone*—had just said something to me that no one else ever had, and I knew my life would never be the same again.

As we reached our bikes, I couldn't resist a last dig at the boys. "Hey, next time you two get the urge to investigate some creepy old building . . . *don't*, okay?"

They promised.

THE MAN WHO
DREW CATS
MICHAEL MARSHALL SMITH

TOM WAS A very tall man, so tall he didn't even have a nickname for it. Ned Black, who was at least a head shorter, had been "Tower Block" since the sixth grade, and Jack had a sign up over the door saying MIND YOUR HEAD, NED. But Tom was just Tom. It was like he was so tall it didn't bear mentioning even for a joke: be a bit like ragging someone for breathing.

Course there were other reasons too for not ragging Tom about his height or anything else. The guys you'll find perched on stools round Jack's Bar watching the game and buying beers, they've known each other forever. Gone to Miss Stadler's school together, gotten under each other's mom's feet, double-dated right up to giving each other's best man's speech. Kingstown is a small place, you understand, and the old boys who come regular to Jack's mostly spent their childhoods in the same tree house. Course they'd since gone their separate ways, up to a point: Pete was an accountant now, had a small office down Union Street just off the Square and did pretty good, whereas Ned was still pumping gas and changing oil and after forty years he did that pretty good too. Comes a time when men have known each other so long they forget what they do for a living most the time, because it just don't matter. When you talk there's a little bit of skimming stones down the quarry in second grade, a whisper of dolling up to go to that first dance, a tad of going to the housewarming when they moved ten years back. There's all that, so much more than you can say, and none of it's important except for having happened.

So we'll stop by and have a couple of beers and talk about the town and rag each other, and the pleasure's just in shooting the breeze and it don't really matter what's said, just the fact that we're all still there to say it.

But Tom, he was different. We all remember the first time we saw him. It was a long hot summer like we haven't seen in the ten years since, and we were lolling under the fans at Jack's and complaining about the tourists. Kingstown does get its share in the summer, even though it's not near the sea and we don't have a McDonald's and I'll be damned if I can figure out why folk'll go out of their way to see what's just a quiet little town near some mountains. It was as hot as Hell that afternoon and as much as a man could do to sit in his shirtsleeves and drink the coolest beer he could find, and Jack's is the coolest for us, and always will be, I guess.

Then Tom walked in. His hair was already pretty white back then, and long, and his face was brown and tough with gray eyes like diamonds set in leather. He was dressed mainly in black with a long coat that made you hot just to look at it, but he looked comfortable like he carried his very own weather around with him and he was just fine.

He got a beer, and sat down at a table and read the town *Bugle*, and that was that.

It was special because there wasn't anything special about it. Jack's Bar isn't exactly exclusive and we don't all turn round and stare at anyone new if they come in, but that place is like a monument to shared times. If a tourist couple comes in out of the heat and sits down, nobody says anything—and maybe nobody even notices at the front of their mind—but it's like there's a little island of the alien in the water and the currents just don't ebb and flow the way they usually do, if you get what I mean. Tom just walked in and sat down and it was all right because it was like he was there just like we were, and could've been for thirty years. He sat and read his paper like part of the same river, and everyone just carried on downstream the way they were.

Pretty soon he goes up for another beer and a few of us got talking to him. We got his name and what he did—painting, he said—and after that it was just shooting the breeze. That quick. He came in that summer afternoon and just fell into the conversation like he'd been there all his life, and sometimes it was hard to imagine he hadn't been. Nobody knew where he came from, or where he'd been, and there was something real quiet about him. A stillness, a man in a slightly different world. But he showed enough to get along real well with us, and a bunch of old friends don't often let someone in like that.

Anyway, he stayed that whole summer. Rented himself a place just round the corner from the square, or so he said: I never saw it. I guess no one did. He was a private man, private like a steel door with four bars and a couple of six-inch padlocks, and when he left the square at the end of the day he could have vanished as soon as he turned the corner for all we knew. But he always came from that direction in the morning, with his easel on his back and paint box under his arm, and he always wore that black coat like it was a part of him. But he always looked cool, and the funny thing was when you stood near him you could swear you felt cooler yourself. I remember Pete saying over a beer that it wouldn't surprise him none if, assuming it ever rained again, Tom would walk round in his own column of dryness. He was just joking, of course, but Tom made you think things like that.

Jack's Bar looks right out onto the square, the kind of square towns don't have much anymore: big and dusty with old roads out each corner, tall shops and houses on all the sides, and some stone paving in the middle round a fountain that ain't worked in living memory. Well in the summer that old square is just full of out-of-towners in pink toweling jumpsuits and nasty jackets standing round saying "Wow" and taking pictures of our quaint old hall and our quaint old stores and even our quaint old selves if we stand still too long. Tom would sit out near the fountain and paint and those people would stand and watch for hours—but he didn't paint the houses or the square or the old Picture House. He painted animals, and painted them like you've never seen. Birds with huge blue speckled wings and cats with cutting green eyes; and whatever he painted it looked like it was just coiled up on the canvas ready to fly away. He didn't do them in their normal colors, they were all reds and purples and deep blues and greens—and yet they fair sparkled with life. It was a wonder to watch: he'd put up a fresh paper, sit looking at nothing in particular, then dip his brush into his paint and draw a line, maybe red, maybe blue. Then he'd add another, maybe the same color, maybe not. Stroke by stroke you could see the animal build up in front of your eyes and yet when it was finished you couldn't believe it hadn't always been there. When he'd finished he'd spray it with some stuff to fix the paints and put a price on it and you can believe me those paintings were sold before they hit the ground. Spreading businessmen from New Jersey or some such and their bored wives would come alive for maybe the first time in years, and walk away with one of those paintings and their arms round each other, looking like they'd found a bit of something they'd forgotten they'd lost.

Come about six o'clock Tom would finish up and walk across to Jack's, looking like a sailing ship among rowing boats and saying yes, he'd be back again tomorrow and yes, he'd be happy to do a painting for them. He'd get a beer and sit with us and watch the game and there'd be no paint on his fingers or his clothes, not a spot. I figured he'd got so much control over that paint it went where it was told and nowhere else.

I asked him once how he could bear to let those paintings go. I know if I'd been able to make anything that good in my whole life I couldn't let it out of my sight, I'd want to keep it to look at sometimes. He thought for a moment and then he said he believed it depends how much of yourself you've put into it. If you've gone deep down and pulled up what's inside and put it down, then you don't want to let it go: you want to keep it, so's you can check sometimes that it's still safely tied down. Comes a time when a painting's so right and so good that it's private, and no one'll understand it except the man who put it down. Only he is going to know what he's talking about. But the everyday paintings, well they were mainly just because he liked to paint animals, and liked for people to have them. He could only put a piece of himself into something he was going to sell, but they paid for the beers and I guess it's like us fellows in Jack's Bar: if you like talking, you don't always have to be saying something important.

Why animals? Well if you'd seen him with them I guess you wouldn't have to ask. He loved them, is all, and they loved him right back. The cats were always his favorites. My old Pa used to say that cats weren't nothing but sleeping machines put on the Earth to do some of the human's sleeping for them, and whenever Tom worked in the square there'd always be a couple curled up near his feet. And whenever he did a chalk drawing, he'd always do a cat.

Once in a while, you see, Tom seemed to get tired of painting on paper, and he'd get out some chalks and sit down on the baking flagstones and just do a drawing right there on the dusty rock. Now I've told you about his paintings, but these drawings were something else again. It was like because they couldn't be bought but would be washed away, he was putting more of himself into it, doing more than just shooting the breeze. They were just chalk on dusty stone and they were still in these weird colors, but I tell you children wouldn't walk near them because they looked so real, and they weren't the only ones, either. People would stand a few feet back and stare and you could see the wonder in their eyes. If they could've been bought there were people who would have sold their houses. I'm telling you. And it's a funny thing but a couple of times when I walked over to open the store up in the mornings I saw a dead bird or two on top of those drawings, almost like they had landed on it and been so terrified to find themselves right on top of a cat they'd dropped dead of fright. But they must have been dumped there by some real cat, of course, because some of those birds looked like they'd been mauled a bit. I used to throw them in the bushes to tidy up and some of them were pretty broken up.

Old Tom was a godsend to a lot of mothers that summer, who found they could leave their little ones by him: do their shopping in peace and have a soda with their friends and come back to find the kids still sitting quietly watching Tom paint. He didn't mind them at all and would talk to them and make them laugh, and kids of that age laughing is one of the best sounds there is. It's the kind of sound that makes the trees grow. They're young and curious and the world spins round them and when they laugh the world seems a brighter place because it takes you back to the time when you knew no evil and everything was good, or if it wasn't, it would be over by tomorrow.

And here I guess I've finally come down to it, because there was one little boy who didn't laugh much, but just sat quiet and watchful, and I guess he probably understands more of what happened that summer than any of us, though maybe not in words he could tell.

His name was Billy McNeill, and he was Jim Valentine's kid. Jim used to be a mechanic, worked with Ned up at the gas station and raced beat-up cars after hours. Which is why his kid is called McNeill now: one Sunday Jim took a corner a mite too fast and the car rolled and the gas tank caught and they never did find all the wheels. A year later his Mary married again. God alone knows why, her folks warned her, her friends warned her, but I guess love must just have been blind. Sam McNeill's work schedule was at best pretty empty, and mostly he just drank and hung out with friends who maybe weren't always this side of the law. I guess Mary had her own sad little miracle and got her sight back pretty soon, because it wasn't long before Sam got free with his fists when the evenings got too long and he'd had a lot too many. You didn't see Mary around much anymore. In these parts people tend to stare at black eyes on a woman, and a deaf man could hear the whisperings of "We Told Her So."

One morning Tom was sitting painting as usual, and little Billy was sitting watching him. Usually he just wandered off after a while but this morning Mary was at the doctor's and she came over to collect him, walking quickly with her face lowered. But not low enough. I was watching from the store, it was kind of a slow day. Tom's face never showed much. He was a man for a quiet smile and a raised eyebrow, but he looked shocked that morning. Mary's eyes were puffed and purple and there was a cut on her cheek an inch long. I guess we'd sort of gotten used to seeing her like that and, if the truth be known, some of the wives thought she'd got remarried a bit on the soon side and I suppose we may all have been a bit cold toward her, Jim Valentine having been so well-liked and all.

Tom looked from the little boy who never laughed much, to his mom with her tired, unhappy eyes and her beat-up face, and his own face went from shocked to stony and I can't describe it any other way but that I felt a cold chill cross my heart from right across the square.

But then he smiled and ruffled Billy's hair and Mary took Billy's hand and they went off. They turned back once and Tom was still looking after them and he gave Billy a little wave, and he waved back and mother and child smiled together.

That night in Jack's Tom put a quiet question about Mary and we told him the story. As he listened his face seemed to harden from within, his eyes growing flat and dead. We told him that old Lou Lachance, who lived next door to the McNeill's, said that sometimes you could hear him shouting and her pleading till three in the morning and on still nights the sound of Billy crying for even longer than that. Told him it was a shame, but what could you do? Folks keep themselves out of other people's faces round here, and I guess Sam and his drinking buddies didn't have much to fear from nearly retireders like us anyhow. Told him it was a terrible thing, and none of us liked it, but these things happened and what could you do.

Tom listened and didn't say a word. Just sat there in his black coat and listened to us pass the buck. After a while the talk sort of petered out and we all sat and watched the bubbles in our beers. I guess the bottom line was that none of us had really thought about it much except as another chapter of small-town gossip, and did I feel ashamed about that by the time we'd finished telling it. Sitting there with Tom was no laughs at all. He had a real edge to him, and seemed more unknown than known that night. He stared at his laced fingers for a long time, and then he began, real slow, to talk.

He'd been married once, he said, a long time ago, and he'd lived in a place called Stevensburg with his wife Rachel. When he talked about her the air seemed to go softer and we all sat quiet and supped our beers and remembered how it had been way back when we first loved our own wives. He talked of her smile and the look in her eyes and when we went home that night I guess there were a few wives who were surprised at how tight they got hugged, and who went to sleep in their husband's arms feeling more loved and contented than they had in a long while.

He'd loved her and she him and for a few years they were the happiest people on earth. Then a third party had got involved. Tom didn't say his name, and he spoke real neutrally about him, but it was a gentleness like silk wrapped round a knife. Anyway his wife fell in love with him, or thought she had. As Tom spoke these words some of us looked up at him, startled, like we'd been slapped across the face.

Rachel did what so many do and live to regret till their dying day. She was so mixed up and getting so much pressure from the other guy that she decided to plough on with the one mistake and make it the biggest in the world.

She left Tom. He talked with her, pleaded even. It was almost impossible to imagine Tom ever doing that, but I guess the man we knew was a different guy from the one he was remembering. The pleading made no difference.

And so Tom had to carry on living in Stevensburg, walking the same tracks, seeing them around, wondering if she was as free and easy with him, if the light in her eyes was shining on him now. And each time the man saw Tom he'd look straight at him and crease a little smile, a grin that said he knew about the pleading and he and his cronies had had a good laugh—and yes, I'm going home with your wife tonight and you want to compare notes?

And then he'd turn and kiss Rachel on the mouth, his eyes on Tom, smiling. And she let him do it.

It had kept gossiping old women in stories for weeks, the way Tom kept losing weight and his temper and the will to live. He took three months of it and then left without bothering to sell the house. Stevensburg was where he'd grown up and courted and loved and now wherever he turned the good times had rotted and hung like fly-blown corpses in all the cherished places. He'd never been back.

It took an hour to tell, and then he stopped talking and Pete got us all some more beers. We were sitting sad and thoughtful, tired like we'd lived it ourselves. And I guess most of us had, some little bit of it. But had we ever loved anyone the way he'd loved her? I doubt it, not all of us put together. Pete set the beers down and Ned asked Tom why he hadn't just beaten the living hell out of the guy. Now, no one else would have actually asked that, but Ned's a good guy, and I guess we were all with him in feeling a piece of that oldest and most crushing hatred in the world, the hate of a man who's lost the woman he loves to another, and we knew what Ned was saying. I'm not saying it's a good thing and I know you're not supposed to feel like that these days but show me a man who says he doesn't and I'll show you a liar. Love is the only feeling worth a tin nickel but you've got to know that it comes from both sides of a man's character and the deeper it runs the darker the pools it draws from.

My guess is he just hated the man too much to hit him. Comes a time when that isn't enough, when nothing is ever going to be enough, and so you can't do anything at all. And as he talked the pain just flowed out like a river that wasn't ever going to be stopped, a river that had cut a channel through every corner of his soul. I learnt something that night that you can go your whole life without realizing: that there are things that can be done that can mess someone up so badly, for so long, that they just cannot be allowed; that there are some kinds of pain that you cannot suffer to be brought into the world.

And then Tom was done telling and he raised a smile and said that in the end he hadn't done anything to the man except paint him a picture, which I didn't understand, but Tom looked like he'd talked all he was going to.

So we got some more beers and shot some quiet pool before going home. But I guess we all knew what he'd been talking about.

Billy McNeill was just a child. He should have been dancing through a world like a big funfair full of sunlight and sounds, and instead he went home at night and saw his mom being beaten up by a man with crap for brains who struck out at a good woman because he was too stupid to deal with the world. Most kids go to sleep thinking about bikes and climbing apple trees and skimming stones, and he was lying there hearing the shouting, and things breaking, and his mother quietly sobbing when it was over. Tom didn't say any of that, but he did. And we knew he was right.

The summer kept up bright and hot, and we all had our businesses to attend to. Jack sold a lot of beer and I sold a lot of ice cream (Sorry ma'am, just the three flavors, and no, Bubblegum Pistachio ain't one of them) and Ned fixed a whole bunch of cracked radiators. Tom sat right out there in the square with a couple of cats by his feet and a crowd around him, magicking up animals in the sun.

And I think that after that night Mary maybe got a few more smiles as she did her shopping, and maybe a few more wives stopped to talk to her. She looked a lot better too: Sam had a job by the sound of it and her face healed up pretty soon. You could often see her standing holding Billy's hand as they watched Tom paint for a while before they went home. I think she realized they had a friend in him. Sometimes Billy was there all afternoon, and he was happy there in the sun by Tom's feet and oftentimes he'd pick up a piece of chalk and sit scrawling on the pavement. Sometimes I'd see Tom lean over and say something to him and he'd look up and smile a simple child's smile that beamed in the sunlight. The tourists kept coming and the sun kept shining and it was one of those summers that go on forever and stick in a child's mind and tell you what summer should be like for the rest of your life. And I'm damn sure it sticks in Billy's mind, just like it does in all of ours.

Because one morning Mary didn't come into the store, which had gotten to being a regular sort of thing, and Billy wasn't out there in the square. After the way things had been the last few weeks that could only be bad news, and so I left the boy John in charge of the store and hurried over to have a word with Tom. I was kind of worried.

I was no more than halfway across to him when I saw Billy come running from the opposite corner of the square, going straight to Tom. He was crying fit to burst and just leapt up at Tom and clung to him, his arms wrapped tight round his neck. Then his mother came across from the same direction, running as best she could. She got to Tom and they just looked at each other. Mary's a real pretty girl but you wouldn't have believed it then. It looked like he'd actually broken her nose this time, and blood was streaming out of her lip. She started sobbing, saying Sam had lost his job because he was back on the drink and what could she do and then suddenly there was a roar and I was shoved aside and Sam was standing there, still wearing his slippers, weaving back and forth and radiating that aura of violence that keeps men like him safe. He started shouting at Mary to take the kid back home and she just flinched and cowered closer to Tom like she was huddling round a fire to keep out the cold. This just got Sam even wilder and he staggered forward and told Tom to get out of it if he knew what was good for him, and grabbed Mary's arm and tried to yank her toward him, his face terrible with rage.

Then Tom stood up. Now Tom was a tall man, but he wasn't a young man, and he was thin. Sam was thirty and built like the town hall. When he did work it usually involved moving heavy things from one place to another, and his strength was supercharged by a whole pile of drunken nastiness.

But at that moment the crowd stepped back as one and I suddenly felt very afraid for Sam McNeill. Tom looked like you could take anything you cared to him and it would just break, like he was a huge spike of granite wrapped in skin with two holes in the face where the rock showed through. And he was mad, not hot and blowing like Sam, but mad and *cold*.

There was a long pause. Then Sam weaved back a step and shouted:

"You just come on home, you hear? Gonna be real trouble if you don't, Mary. Real trouble," and then he stormed off across the square the way he came, knocking his way through the tourist vultures soaking up the spicy local color.

Mary turned to Tom, so afraid it hurt to see, and said she guessed she'd better be going. Tom looked at her for a moment and then spoke for the first time.

"Do you love him?"

Even if you wanted to, you ain't going to lie to eyes like that, for fear something inside you will break.

Real quiet she said, "No," and began crying softly as she took Billy's hand and walked slowly back across the square.

Tom packed up his stuff and walked over to Jack's. I went with him and had a beer but I had to get back to the shop and Tom just sat there like a trigger, silent and strung up tight as a drum. Somewhere down near the bottom of those still waters something was stirring. Something I thought I didn't want to see.

About an hour later it was lunchtime and I'd just left the shop to have a break when suddenly something whacked into the back of my legs and nearly knocked me down. It was Billy. It was Billy and he had a bruise round his eye that was already closing it up.

I knew what the only thing to do was and I did it. I took his hand and led him across to Jack's Bar, feeling a hard anger pushing against my throat. When he saw Tom, Billy ran to him again and Tom took him in his arms and looked over Billy's shoulder at me, and I felt my own anger collapse utterly in the face of a fury I could never have generated. I tried to find a word to describe it but they all just seemed like they were in the wrong language. All I can say is I wanted to be somewhere else and it felt real cold standing there facing that stranger in a black coat.

Then the moment passed and Tom was holding the kid close, ruffling his hair and talking to him in a low voice, murmuring the words I thought only mothers knew. He dried Billy's tears and checked his eye and then he got off his stool, smiled down at him and said:

"I think it's time we did some drawing, what d'you say?" and, taking the kid's hand, he picked up his chalk box and walked out into the square.

I don't know how many times I looked up and watched them that afternoon. They were sitting side by side on the stone, Billy's little hand wrapped round

one of Tom's fingers, and Tom doing one of his chalk drawings. Every now and then Billy would reach across and add a little bit and Tom would smile and say something and Billy's gurgling laugh would float across the square. The store was real busy that afternoon and I was chained to that counter, but I could tell by the size of the crowd that a lot of Tom was going into that picture, and maybe a bit of Billy too.

It was about four o'clock before I could take a break. I walked across the crowded square in the mid-afternoon heat and shouldered my way through to where they sat with a couple of cold Cokes. And when I saw it my mouth just dropped open and took a five-minute vacation while I tried to take it in.

It was a cat all right, but not a normal cat. It was a life-size tiger. I'd never seen Tom do anything near that big before, and as I stood there in the beating sun trying to get my mind round it, it almost seemed to stand in three dimensions, a nearly living thing. Its stomach was very lean and thin, its tail seemed to twitch with color, and as Tom worked on the eyes and jaws, his face set with a rigid concentration quite unlike his usual calm painting face, the snarling mask of the tiger came to life before my eyes. And I could see that he wasn't just putting a bit of himself in at all. This was a man at full stretch, giving all of himself and reaching down for more, pulling up bloody fistfuls and throwing them down. The tiger was all the rage I'd seen in his eyes, and more, and like his love for Rachel that rage just seemed bigger than any other man could comprehend. He was pouring it out and sculpting it into the lean and ravenous creature coming to pulsating life in front of us on the pavement, and the weird purples and blues and reds just made it seem more vibrant and alive.

I watched him working furiously on it, the boy sometimes helping, adding a tiny bit here and there that strangely seemed to add to it, and thought I understood what he'd meant that evening a few weeks back. He said he'd done a painting for the man who'd given him so much pain. Then, as now, he must have found what I guess you'd call something fancy like "catharsis" through his skill with chalks, had wrenched the pain up from within him and nailed it down onto something solid that he could walk away from. Now he was helping that little boy do the same, and the boy did look better, his bruised eye hardly showing with the wide smile on his face as he watched the big cat conjured up from nowhere in front of him.

We all just stood and watched, like something out of an old story, the simple folk and the magical stranger. It always feels like you're giving a bit of yourself away when you praise someone else's creation, and its often done grudgingly, but you could feel the awe that day like a warm wind. Comes a time when you realize something special is happening, something you're never going to see again, and there isn't anything you can do but watch.

Well I had to go back to the store after a while. I hated to go but, well, John is a good boy, married now of course, but in those days his head was full of girls and it didn't do to leave him alone in a busy shop for too long.

And so the long hot day drew slowly to a close. I kept the store open till eight, when the light began to turn and the square emptied out with all the tourists going away to write postcards and see if we didn't have even just a *little* McDonald's hidden away someplace. I suppose Mary had troubles enough at home, realized where the boy would be and figured he was safer there than anywhere else, and I guess she was right.

Tom and Billy finished up drawing and then Tom sat and talked to him for some time. Then they got up and the kid walked slowly off to the corner of the square, looking back to wave at Tom a couple times. Tom stood and watched him go and when Billy had gone he stayed there a while, head down, like a huge black statue in the gathering dark. He looked kind of creepy out there and I don't mind telling you I was glad when he finally moved and started walking over toward Jack's. I ran out to catch up with him and drew level just as we passed the drawing. And then I had to stop. I just couldn't look at that and move at the same time.

Finished, the drawing was like nothing on earth, and I suppose that's exactly what it was. I can't hope to describe it to you, although I've seen it in my dreams many times in the last ten years. You had to be there, on that heavy summer night, had to know what was going on. Otherwise it's going to sound like it was just a drawing.

That tiger was out and out terrifying. It looked so mean and hungry, I don't know what: it just looked like the darkest parts of mankind, the pain and the fury and the vengeful hate nailed down in front of you for you to see, and I just stood there and shivered in the humid evening air.

"We did him a picture," Tom said quietly.

"Yeah," I said, and nodded. Like I said, I know what "catharsis" means and I thought I understood what he was saying. But I really didn't want to look at it much longer. "Let's go have a beer, hey?"

The storm in Tom hadn't passed, I could tell, and he still seemed to thrum with crackling emotions looking for an earth, but I thought the clouds might be breaking and I was glad.

And so we walked slowly over to Jack's and had a few beers and watched some pool being played. Tom seemed pretty tired, but still alert, and I relaxed a little. Come eleven most of the guys started going on their way and I was surprised to see Tom get another beer.

Pete, Ned, and I stayed on, and Jack of course, though we knew our loving wives would have something to say about that. It just didn't seem time to go. Outside it had gotten pretty dark, though the moon was keeping the square in a kind of twilight and the lights in the bar threw a pool of warmth out of the front window.

Then, about twelve o'clock, it happened, and I don't suppose any of us will ever see the same world we grew up in again. I've told this whole thing like it was just me who was there, but we all were, and we remember it together.

Because suddenly there was a wailing sound outside, a thin cutting cry, getting closer. Tom immediately snapped to his feet and stared out the window like he'd been waiting for it. As we looked out across the square we saw little Billy come running and we could see the blood on his face from there. Some of us got to get up but Tom snarled at us to stay there and so I guess we just stayed put, sitting back down like we'd been pushed. He strode out the door and into the square and the boy saw him and ran to him and Tom folded him in his cloak and held him close and warm. But he didn't come back in. He just stood there, and he was waiting for something.

Now there's a lot of crap talked about silences. I read novels when I've the time and you see things like "Time stood still" and so on and you think no way it did. So

I'll just say I don't think anyone in the world breathed in that next minute. There was no wind, no movement. The stillness and silence were there like you could touch them, but more than that: they were like that's all there was and all there ever had been.

We felt the slow red throb of violence from right across the square before we could even see the man. Then Sam came staggering into view waving a bottle like a flag and cursing his head off. At first he couldn't see Tom and the boy because they were the opposite side of the fountain, and he ground to a wavering halt, but then he started shouting, rough jags of sound that seemed to strike against the silence and die instead of breaking it, and he began charging across the square—and if ever there was a man with murder in his thoughts then it was Sam McNeill. He was like a man who'd given his soul the evening off. I wanted to shout to Tom to get the hell out of the way, to come inside, but the words wouldn't come out of my throat and we all just stood there, knuckles whitening as we clutched the bar and stared, our mouths open like we'd made a pact never to use them again. Tom just stood there, watching Sam come toward him, getting closer, almost as far as the spot where Tom usually painted. It felt like we were looking out of the window at a picture of something that happened long ago in another place and time, and the closer Sam got the more I began to feel very afraid for him.

It was at that moment that Sam stopped dead in his tracks, skidding forward like in some kid's cartoon, his shout dying off in his ragged throat. He was staring at the ground in front of him, his eyes wide and his mouth a stupid circle. Then he began to scream.

It was a high shrill noise like a woman's, and coming out of that bull of a man it sent fear racking down my spine. He started making thrashing movements like he was trying to move backward, but he just stayed where he was.

His movements became unmistakable at about the same time his screams turned from terror to agony. He was trying to get his leg away from something.

Suddenly he seemed to fall forward on one knee, his other leg stuck out behind him, and he raised his head and shrieked at the dark skies and we saw his face then and I'm not going to forget that face so long as I live. It was a face from before there were any words, the face behind our oldest fears and earliest nightmares, the face we're terrified of seeing on ourselves one night when we're alone in the dark and It finally comes out from under the bed to get us, like we always knew it would.

Then Sam fell on his face, his leg buckled up—and still he thrashed and screamed and clawed at the ground with his hands, blood running from his broken fingernails as he twitched and struggled. Maybe the light was playing tricks, and my eyes were sparkling anyway on account of being too paralyzed with fear to even blink, but as he thrashed less and less it became harder and harder to see him at all, and as the breeze whipped up stronger his screams began to sound a lot like the wind. But still he writhed and moaned and then suddenly there was the most godawful crunching sound and then there was no movement or sound anymore.

Like they were on a string our heads all turned together and we saw Tom still standing there, his coat flapping in the wind. He had a hand on Billy's shoulder and as we looked we could see that Mary was there too now and he had one arm round her as she sobbed into his coat.

I don't know how long we just sat there staring but then we were ejected off our seats and out of the bar. Pete and Ned ran to Tom but Jack and I went to where Sam had fallen, and we stared down, and I tell you the rest of my life now seems like a build up to and a climb down from that moment.

We were standing in front of a chalk drawing of a tiger. Even now my scalp seems to tighten when I think of it, and my chest feels like someone punched a hole in it and tipped a gallon of ice water inside. I'll just tell you the facts: Jack was there and he knows what we saw and what we didn't see.

What we didn't see was Sam McNeill. He just wasn't there. We saw a drawing of a tiger in purples and greens, a little bit scuffed, and there was a lot more red round the mouth of that tiger than there had been that afternoon, and I'm sure that if either of us could have dreamed of reaching out and touching it, it would have been warm too.

And the hardest part to tell is this. I'd seen that drawing in the afternoon, and Jack had too, and we knew that when it was done it was lean and thin.

I swear to God that tiger wasn't thin anymore. What Jack and I were looking at was one fat tiger.

After a while I looked up and across at Tom. He was still standing with Mary and Billy, but they weren't crying anymore. Mary was hugging Billy so tight he squawked and Tom's face looked calm and alive and creased with a smile. And as we stood there the skies opened for the first time in months and a cool rain hammered down. At my feet colors began to run and lines became less distinct. Jack and I stood and watched till there was just pools of meaningless colors and then we walked slowly over to the others, not even looking at the bottle lying on the ground, and we all stayed there a long time in the rain, facing each other, not saying a word.

Well that was ten years ago, near enough. After a while Mary took Billy home and they turned to give us a little wave before they turned the corner. The cuts on Billy's face healed real quick, and he's a good-looking boy now: he looks a lot like his dad and he's already fooling about in cars. Helps me in the store sometimes. His mom ain't aged a day and looks wonderful. She never married again, but she looks real happy the way she is.

The rest of us just said a simple goodnight. Goodnight was all we could muster and maybe that's all there was to say. Then we walked off home in the directions of our wives. Tom gave me a small smile before he turned and walked off alone. I almost followed him, I wanted to say something, but in the end I just stayed where I was and watched him go. And that's how I'll always remember him best, because for a moment there was a spark in his eyes and I knew that some pain had been lifted deep down inside somewhere.

Then he walked and no one has seen him since, and like I said it's been about ten years now. He wasn't there in the square the next morning and he didn't come in for a beer. Like he'd never been, he just wasn't there. Except for the hole in our hearts: it's funny how much you can miss a quiet man.

We're all still here, of course, Jack, Ned, Pete, and the boys, and all much the same, though even older and grayer. Pete lost his wife and Ned retired but things go on the same. The tourists come in the summer and we sit on the stools and drink our cold beers and shoot

the breeze about ballgames and families and how the
world's going to crap, and sometimes we'll draw close
and talk about a night a long time ago, and about paintings and cats, and about the quietest man we ever knew,
wondering where he is, and what he's doing. And we've
had a six-pack of beer in the back of the fridge for ten
years now, and the minute he walks through that door
and pulls up a stool, that's his.

ARE YOU AFRAID
OF THE DARK?
CHARLES L. GRANT

THE STORM BEGAN moving just below the hori-
zon, setting houses and trees in sharp silhouette,
freezing the clouds in gray and roiling white; it buried the sunset and drove off the stars and replaced the
moon's shadows with strobic shadows of its own.

Yet it was harmless out there, far enough away to
make people smile, glance at their watches, and walk
only a bit faster. There was no warning in the forecast,
and its own warning was muttered, softened by the
spring air that just an hour ago filled with sun and new
flowers and leaves brilliant green on the trees along
the curbs.

Then the breeze became a wind, and the storm turned around, a panther stalking the night with flashes of lightning where its claws touched the ground, grumblings of thunder when it spotted its prey.

The breeze became a wind, and the temperature dropped, and all that was left was the waiting for the rain.

The padded deacon's bench had been turned around to face the picture window in the den. The floral draperies had been pulled back, the lights had been turned off, and the backyard was visible only between the blinks of an eye, as the storm moved overhead and crashed down on the house. Lightning escaped the confines of black clouds, flaring, crackling, giving the trees angled movement and turning the back hedge into a huge black wall. The ornamental wishing well, the birdbath, the toolshed in the corner, all of them curiously flat when the air burned blue-white ahead of the thunder. The leaves were silver, the grass pale-gray, and the reflections in the pane were bloodless and transparent.

"She's right," Jeremy Kneale said, squirming on the bench but not wanting to leave. "Bernie's right, it's just like a movie."

"It is not. It's stupid. It's dark out, can't you see that?" Stacey flinched at the next lightning bolt, but he still wasn't impressed. "It's dumb. I wanna watch TV."

"Bernie says we can't," Will reminded him. "She says we have to wait until something good comes on."

"Her real name," said Stacey, "is Bernadette, and Bernadette is a real pain in the ass."

Jeremy winced at the way his friend talked about their new babysitter, but he didn't say a word. Scolding Stacey Parsons was a waste of time. He knew that. He had heard his mother tell his father that a hundred times, and heard them wonder how the boy's parents managed without strangling him. That part was a joke; at least, he thought it was a joke.

Behind them, through the swinging door that led into the kitchen, they could hear Bernie working. Making popcorn. Fixing trays. Getting glasses from the cupboard and pouring them soda.

"I feel stupid," Will confessed at last.

Jeremy did too, but he wouldn't admit it. He was in enough trouble already, and the one thing he didn't need was Bernie telling his folks that he was being dif- ficult again. Yet it wasn't his fault. He liked to explore things, go places, find new games to play with his best friends in the whole world. Just because it sometimes got him into trouble with the neighbors, or with people he didn't even know, didn't mean he was bad. Like the window this afternoon at the toy shop. He didn't mean to break it, but Stacey had ducked when he'd tossed the rock at him. Not a throw, just a toss, and it must have hit the pane just right because the next thing they knew there was glass all over the pavement and lots of big people reaching for them so they wouldn't run away.

It was an accident.

His parents didn't believe him.

And parents, Stacey had said once, never believed the kid when there was a grownup around. You had to be big to be believed; you had to be able to defend yourself with something else besides tears.

"I'm hungry," Will Young said, standing and walking away from the window. He turned on a lamp, blinking at the light.

"Yeah," said Stacey. He stood, gestured, and he and Jeremy turned the bench around where it belonged. Then he closed the drapes and sat again, hands in his lap, feet swinging. "I wish she'd hurry up."

"It's like prison," Will said, rubbing his hands together and grinning. "Bernie is the guard, see, and our parents are off to see the governor, to find out when they're going to throw the switch."

"Where'd you hear that?" Jeremy asked.

"Saw it in a movie."

Jeremy shook his head. "I saw that movie, and you got it wrong. They're supposed to find out if the governor is going to stop them from throwing the switch."

"Sure," Stacey said. "Did you see the look on my father's face when he found out what happened today?"

He shuddered. "I know that look. He's gonna be right there by the guy with the black mask. He's gonna throw the switch himself."

Jeremy had to agree. He had never seen any of their parents so angry before. As if he and his buddies had deliberately set out to find trouble, or cause it when they couldn't find it, and lied about it when they did. Of course, they didn't always tell the truth because then they'd really get clobbered. As it was, they were supposed to stay on their own property for a whole two weeks, and the only reason they were allowed together tonight was because his father had decided it was time the six grownups got together and decided what to do about taming their hellions.

He didn't know exactly what *hellions* meant when he heard his father on the phone with Mr. Young the other night, but he did know it wasn't good. And he knew that this time they weren't going to be able to cry or beg or pout their way out of whatever punishment there was going to be. Staying home wasn't punishment; staying home was only getting ready for whatever big stuff was coming after.

Lightning; and thunder.

Ashes in the fireplace shifting into piles.

The wind rattling the pane and keening through the eaves.

The boys jumped, smiled nervously, and jumped again when the kitchen door pushed open and Bernie came out with a tray in her hands. She walked to the card table in the middle of the room and put the tray in the center. There were three glasses filled with soda, a huge bowl of popcorn, and three chocolate candy bars.

None of the boys moved. They only watched as the babysitter frowned at the closed drapes, at the turned-around bench, and at Will still standing by the floor lamp in the corner. Her short brown hair seemed darker tonight, her eyes deeper, her nose sharper, and when she brushed her hands down the side of her dress, she seemed less like a friend than the guard Will had described.

"I thought," she said, "you were going to watch the storm."

"That's dumb," Stacey told her.

"Yeah," Will agreed.

She turned to Jeremy then and waited for his answer.

He shrugged. He didn't want to get her mad, didn't want her to tell his mother and father he was being a pain again. Bernie was all right, and he wanted to keep her on his side. She had stayed with him twice before, and with Stacey and Will too, just after the big trouble started, and though she sometimes made him nervous the way she looked at him, the way she walked around the house without making a sound, he thought she was pretty okay, for a grownup.

"Sit," she said, and pointed at the bench.

They did, sensing something in her manner that forestalled rebellion. Besides, they could smell the butter on the popcorn, see the bubbles in the soda, and the chocolate bars were the largest they had ever seen in their lives.

"We're going to have a contest," she told them, standing behind the table with her hands folded at her waist. "It's going to be a lot of fun. The only thing is, you can't be afraid."

"Afraid?" Stacey said. "Who's afraid?"

Bernie smiled slowly. "Aren't you scared of the dark?"

Stacey laughed, Will sneered, Jeremy pulled on his ear.

She stared at them until Will giggled. "Stace is scared of the ocean," he said, taking a punch on the arm.

"Yeah? Well, you're scared of the dark, you even still got a nightlight."

Jeremy kept silent—he was only scared of his parents.

"Good," she said. "That's fine, because the contest, you see, is a series of games that I pick for you to play."

"Big deal," said Will, poking Jeremy in the ribs.

"What is it, spin the bottle?" Stacey said, laughing until he saw the look on her face.

"Thank you," she said. "Now pay attention, please. I want you to listen closely. Since you're not afraid of the dark, I'll pick something . . ." She looked to the ceiling, looked down, and touched the table. "If you get scared, you lose."

"Jesus, Bernie," Stacey said. "We're not babies, you know."

"I know," she told him. "And that's what I told your parents. You're not babies anymore. You can take it. You're tough."

"Right," Stacey said, Will nodded emphatically, and Jeremy said, "Take what?"

Bernie ignored him. "The rules are simple: I pick the games, nobody quits before the end, and for every game you win you get to keep a bar of this chocolate."

"That's not fair," Stacey complained.

Bernie smiled. "Second place gets popcorn."

"Hey!" said Will.

"And last place gets to sleep in the rain."

Jeremy looked at his friends, looked at Bernie, and decided that this wasn't going to be a good night after all.

She looked at her watch. "We'd better get started. I promised your parents we'd be done before they return. Are you ready?"

They each nodded, staring at the chocolate bars each weighing three pounds.

"In that case," she said, in the thunder, in the lightning, while the wind knocked on the door, "the first game is:"

hide-and-seek

It was dark, so dark it was like living in a black cloud.

And it was quiet, except for the sound of his breathing.

Will Young closed his mouth and his eyes and wished he wasn't so fat. His mother was always yelling at him for eating too much, and for sneaking food into his bedroom after he was supposed to be asleep. But he didn't care. He enjoyed eating. It didn't matter what there was in the cupboards or in the refrigerator as long as it was good—and there wasn't much he didn't like.

And he didn't think he was really gross-and-ugly fat, not like his father was, with his belly showing even when his shirt was all buttoned. He just had a little extra here and there around his waist and his face, and that definitely didn't stop him from being able to run, or climb, or crawl under the porch; at least his arms didn't have all that flab hanging down, and at least his thighs didn't rub together because there was no room between them.

Nevertheless, he wished now he was a little slimmer, because then he could squeeze a bit further back into the closet, maybe even get behind the golf bag that belonged to Jerry's father. He didn't think he'd have to stay here very long because Stacey said it was a dumb game and didn't want to play and would probably deliberately get himself caught first. Jerry knew the house better than anyone, but Will thought he was scared of something and would probably head right for the cellar, the first place Bernie would look.

The huge closet in the upstairs hall, then, was almost perfect when he found it. Clothes and coats hanging from the rail, boxes and stuff stacked on the floor, and the door so snug no light came underneath it.

He reached out his hands and felt around him, trying to move things in front and move himself farther back, without making any noise. He breathed through his mouth. He froze whenever he heard footsteps passing outside.

And he finally reached the corner after moving the golf bag aside.

Perfect. Dark, but perfect. Bernie would have to declare him the winner of this game, no question about it.

He grinned, and rubbed his hands together.

He pulled his knees up to his chest, and listened to the muffled spill of thunder over the roof.

And heard something move on the other side of the closet.

He blinked and cocked his head, frowning as he listened as hard as he could and wondering what it was, or maybe it was his imagination.

A *scratching*, soft and slow, maybe it's a rat or a bat or something that lives in the back of the closet and waits for dopes like him to play stupid baby games in the middle of a storm; a *scratching*, soft and slow, and something suddenly brushed quickly over his face. He almost yelled as he lashed out to knock it away, nearly yelled again when his fingers were caught, trapped in something that had round hard teeth. His free hand grabbed for it while he pushed deeper into the corner, grabbed and yanked, and something fell over his face.

He did yell, then, but the sound was muffled, all sound deadened as his feet kicked out and struck the golf bag, as his head slammed against the wall, as his hands tore and pulled and the thing dropped and tangled into his lap, and a coat hanger a moment later fell onto his chest.

Crap, he thought as he felt the jacket on his legs, the round buttons, the smooth lapels. Crap, you're a jerk.

He shuddered and rolled his shoulders, wiped a hand over his eyes and felt the perspiration slick on his face. He dried himself with the jacket and pulled the golf bag back in front of him, proud that he'd fought the demons and hadn't been killed.

Besides, this proved that he'd made a good choice. This proved he could be quiet.

Bernie, he knew then, would never find him now. She might open the door, but even the light from the hall wouldn't reach him back here. And she surely wouldn't come in, not with that dress on. He giggled, and quickly covered his mouth. He didn't know her very well, only the two other times he'd been over when she'd sat with Jeremy, but he knew she wouldn't want to dirty that dress. She was very careful about it. He could see that. He could see how she stayed away from the walls, and held the skirt away from anything that might touch it and make it dirty.

She was weird, and not even Jeremy could tell him he was wrong. Weird, and always looking at them as if they were bugs or something. Sometimes she was fun, like with the spooky stories she'd tell them, but most of the time she just sat on the bench in the den and watched them. Like a guard. Like a dog. Until Mr. and Mrs. Kneale came home, and then she would put on her coat and leave without even saying goodnight.

Weird.

Really weird.

And a *scratching* in the corner.

A laugh outside as Stacey ran down the hall, telling his two friends he was caught but don't give up, Bernie was a jerk, and they'd share the chocolate later.

Will smiled and nodded to himself. One down, one to go. All she had to do was find Jeremy and the game was all his. All that candy, all his.

His stomach growled.

Something scratched lightly in the corner, and he wished there wasn't such a draft in here, tickling his neck and making him think there was something crawling through his hair. The wind outside had found a hole in the walls, had snuck around the windows, and now he was getting cold and the clothes were moving and rustling together, whispering to each other and scratching.

are you afraid of the dark?

A monster, he thought then, and squeezed his eyes closed, grateful for the colored lights that swirled in small circles and the curtains of faint orange that drifted down from the top, disappeared and came back; there was a monster in the closet.

He shifted, and heard someone walking the hall outside the door.

Bernie, he called silently, *go find Jeremy, I'm not here.*

A monster in with him, but the candy bars were huge and all he had to do was wait until his best friend was found.

A coat hanger scraped on the metal pole overhead.

Besides, there's no such things as monsters and I will not be afraid because I am hungry and I want that candy, he thought, his hands tight in fists, his eyes still closed.

Something thumped against the golf bag, and the clubs inside rattled.

No such thing. No such thing.

The bag quivered again, and he felt a weight press against the sole of his sneaker. And he sighed his relief, grinned and shook his head at how stupid he could be. It had been his foot all the time. He had unthinkingly stretched a leg out and had kicked the bag with his foot, so there was nothing to worry about, alone here in the dark.

scratching

Then he heard Jeremy running, probably from his bedroom, not the cellar after all, telling Will it was over, that he'd won the first game.

He sighed again, loudly, and nodded. He knew he would win. How could they have thought otherwise? Wasn't he the champion hide-and-seeker in the whole school, if not the whole entire world? Couldn't he do something wrong and then hide from his parents until they were nearly frantic with fear and he popped out and smiled and they forgot they were angry?

Crap, he was the champ. Bernie should have known.

A footstep by the door.

And a *scratching* inside.

He grinned and shifted, and took hold of the bag.

Someone turned the lock . . . turned the lock and walked away.

"Hey," he said. "Hey, Bernie, it's me!"

And he pushed the bag aside, and saw the red eyes staring at him.

The candy bars sat in the middle of the table, and Stacey stood as close as he dared, one eye on Bernie fussing with the logs in the fireplace, the other on the reward he would win the next time. Had Jeremy been last, it would have been different because Jerry was okay. But Will was a p-i-g hog and he didn't think he could stand sitting here watching that pig scoff down all that chocolate.

Bernie rose and dusted her hands on the apron she wore around her waist.

Stacey decided he would win the next one, and let Jerry have the last. At least that way, Will-the-pig wouldn't hog it all and make them look stupid besides.

"Are you ready?" she asked, standing on the hearth.

Jeremy looked toward the stairs that led to the first floor. "But we can't," he said. "We gotta wait for Will."

"The hell with Will," Stacey said with a sneer. "He's got his dumb candy, now he's just playing. We oughta let him stay wherever he is all night."

"That's not fair!"

"If that's the way Will wants it," Bernie said softly, "then that's the way he'll have it. If he's not back before we finish the next game, he'll forfeit his prize."

"Yeah," Stacey said. "Way t'go, Bernie.'

She smiled briefly, and he smiled back. She was really queer, but she had bigger tits even than his mother, and he didn't think she knew that he'd been trying to look down her dress all night. He'd whispered that to Jerry while they were waiting for Will, and the dip had blushed. He really had blushed. Stacey figured the kid didn't know anything about women, and wasn't surprised. His old man was the strictest parent in the world, and wouldn't even let him look at photography magazines. That was dumb. That was really and truly dumb.

"So," he said, "when do we start?"

"Stace . . ."

"Aw, c'mon, huh? They're gonna be back soon. We gotta get a move on."

"Stacey's right," Bernie said. She reached into the apron pocket, then, and pulled out something wrapped in white cloth. Slowly, she pulled the corners aside, and he saw in her palm a massive red jewel. It caught the dim light and doubled it, seemed to quiver when thunder rumbled through the room.

"Wow," he said.

"This," she said, "was taken from a very rich man. He has the police looking for it. He's given them one hour to find it or else." She smiled without showing her teeth. "We're going to play:"

cops and robbers

Stacey knew he had made a mistake. He should have found some place inside to hide the jewel, but had convinced himself that Jerry would have found it in less than ten minutes. After all, it was his house, and he knew all the good places where such a thing could be hidden.

But this was silly.

He stood on the patio, the wind tearing at his hair and lashing it in his face, making him squint, hunching his shoulders, making his arms tremble as he considered digging a hole in one of the potted plants and burying it there.

No. Once Jerry knew he'd left the house, that would be the first place he'd look. And there wasn't time to dig a hole in the yard because the ground was still hard and he didn't have any tools.

Dumb, Parsons, he told himself when the wind turned him around. Really and truly dumb.

Then a streak of cloud-smothered lightning illuminated the backyard, and he grinned so hard his cheeks began to ache.

The well. That stupid plaster well Mrs. Kneale had bought last summer. They were forbidden to go near it, to touch, even to breathe on it, which didn't bother him because he thought it was stupid. What good was a well when it didn't go anywhere? All Mr. Kneale had done was take it out of the station wagon with Jerry and his help, and carried it to the yard, plunked it down, and got himself a beer to celebrate. Mrs. Kneale had applauded like they'd moved the stupid damn Empire State Building, and after that she and Jerry's father would sit on the patio and toss pennies at it, making wishes. She'd wanted Stacey to do it once, and he did because Jerry was his friend, but he'd felt dumb and he made Jerry swear later he wouldn't tell a soul.

Then, in August, he'd had an idea.

Mr. Kneale was getting pretty good at pitching the coins in; he could even do it most times with his eyes closed. So one night, when they were supposed to have been over at Will's, they snuck through the hole in the hedge and moved the well over. Just a few inches, not enough to notice.

Mr. Kneale missed, moved his chair, and recovered his aim.

They moved the well again, back where it was, and sat on the other side of the hedge in Will's yard and laughed themselves into hiccoughs when they heard the guy swearing.

They managed it twice more, until the night Jerry slipped on the damp grass and the well landed hard. One side cracked. A small split they didn't think any-one would notice.

Mrs. Kneale did, and that stupid Jerry broke the minute she asked him if they'd been fooling around.

Stupidass Jerry. Him and his stupidass books and his posters and not even knowing what Bernie looked like without her clothes. Damn, but they'd gotten into a hell of a lot of trouble, especially when Stacey had let slip a bad word when his mother grabbed for his arm. Christ, that had put him in his room for a whole goddamned week.

The well, then. Jerry was still too scared to go near it, and wouldn't dream that his old pal still had the nerve.

He hurried off the patio onto the grass, crouched over and running on his toes, stopping once when lightning put a shadow in front of him and it took him a moment to realize it was his own. A look back over his shoulder, the draperies were still closed, and he dove around the side of the well, out of the wind.

Buried lightning again, and the mutter of thunder, and he whirled around when he thought he heard something coming through the hedge.

Nothing. It was nothing.

The leaves husked and branches rattled, and grass crawled toward his legs, and all the houses he could see were perfectly dark. Holes in the night; mouths of black monsters that ate people after sunset.

"Damn," he said into the wind. It made him feel better, because the wind was getting on his nerves. "Damn, crap, blast, hell." He smiled, and pulled the ruby out of his pocket, lifted his hand to drop it in the well when he stopped, frowned, and wondered just how stupid-dumb Jerry really was. He just might think of the well, he just might, and if he looked inside with a flashlight he'd see it right away and get all the chocolate. Worse; he'd brag about it to every kid in the school, every day for a goddamned year. Worse yet, he'd prove he was such a good little boy that his parents would lift the grounding, and leave Stacey stuck in his room.

What he had to do then was think like a robber, a crook who was going to come back real soon and take the loot and run away once the cops had been by. He nodded to himself, looked back to the toolshed and knew that was too obvious. If he was going to hide it out here, then, he would have to put it in the well, but cover it with something. Grass, maybe some dirt, so the light wouldn't shine off it.

Suddenly, lightning sheered out of the clouds, ripping a hole in the night like a sheet tearing in half. He jumped and clutched the jewel to his stomach, closed his eyes and waited for the thunder.

When it came, cracking the air and smashing over his head, his ears stoppered, and he yelled, jumped to his feet, and stared wide-eyed at the house.

This was nuts. He was going to fry out here, all for a stupid piece of chocolate. Then he put a hand on the plaster lip and looked into the well.

And blinked.

The edge only came to his waist, but it looked like it dropped a hundred miles into the ground. Maybe even a million. Mr. Kneale must've dug a hole under it, to pretend it was real and keep them from playing their trick on him again. He smiled; it was perfect. And he leaned over, reached out his hand, and when lightning flared again he could see all the way to the bottom. To the grass. To the lousy damned grass.

"Well, damn," he said, and without wasting any more time, he hitched himself onto the lip and dropped in.

The wind passing over the mouth sounded like hollow trumpets, and the sides quivered, the peaked roof shook, and the plastic bucket on the chain rocked alarmingly fast. It was a tight fit, but he had plenty of room to dig a small hole between his shoes with his fingers, place the jewel carefully inside, and cover it again. Then he waited for the next bolt to be sure his work couldn't be seen.

When it came, he saw the water, and couldn't stop himself from falling toward the red eyes floating toward him.

This isn't funny anymore, Jeremy thought, but he didn't have the nerve to leave the deacon's bench and complain. Bernie was in the kitchen again, making something on the stove, rattling pans and banging spoons and whistling so far off-key the noise scraped his spine like claws on a blackboard.

This isn't fun.

He looked over his shoulder, out the window to the yard that flicked in and out of his vision, white, black, white again and jumping over the well in the center. He had thought, a few minutes ago, that he'd seen Stacey creeping around there, but when the lightning came again and there was nothing to see, he changed his mind. Stacey was crazy, but not crazy enough for that.

His tongue touched his upper lip.

His left foot tapped on the floor.

He looked to the stairwell when he thought he heard Will, then looked to the back door when he thought he heard Stace.

Then the kitchen door slammed open, and Bernie walked in.

He blinked, and tried to smile, but there was an ice cube settling on the back of his neck, and it grew when he heard the first spattering of rain on the window.

Bernie sat in his father's chair by the fireplace and looked at the charred logs, raised her head and smiled straight at him. Her face was in partial shadow, and he could see only one eye, only one part of the mouth, only a few of her teeth.

"Are you worried about your friends?"

He nodded, and swallowed because he thought he was going to break down and cry, and that was the one thing he'd promised himself he'd never do again. All it ever did was get a slap from his father, or a shout from his mother—act your age, Jeremy Kneale, you're not a baby anymore.

"I wouldn't," she whispered. "They're doing just fine."

"How do you know?" he said, more angrily than he'd intended. "All you do is make that stupid popcorn. Will is hurt somewhere, I just know it. And Stacey must be out there in all that rain." He rose and stood in front of her, hands clenched at his sides, fighting the burning that flushed his cheeks. "You don't care. You just want to get us in trouble again, that's all. Our folks are gonna come home, and we're gonna get in the biggest trouble in the world."

Bernie clasped her hands in her lap and watched the logs again, as if they were burning. "Jeremy, do you know what bog butter is?"

He frowned, looked away, looked back. "What?"

"It's our game, Jeremy. Surely you haven't forgotten the third game. Now answer my question: Have you ever heard of bog butter?"

"I . . ." He felt a tear in his right eye, a lump of coal in his throat. "Huh?"

She smiled dreamily, and sighed. "In the old days, long before there was even a United States, they used to bury people in marshes over in England. You know what a marsh is?"

He nodded.

The rain slapped at the pane, ran over the edge of the gutter, and poured into the shrubs cringing under the window.

"Well, sometimes, when they dug these people up, they found that the bodies had oozed a kind of wax over themselves. It looked a little like butter, I guess, so they called it bog butter."

"That's nice," he said, knowing it sounded stupid, but what else could he say? His friends were lost in the storm and in the house, and Bernie was sitting in his father's chair talking about dead bodies and butter and—god! — he wished she'd shut up so he could talk to her.

"At the time, of course, they didn't know what had caused it, or why it was there."

He edged away, his head ducking, his hips turning before he did. And when she didn't seem to notice, he backed up to the staircase, then flung himself up, racing down the hall to his room on the far end. He checked under the bed, in his closet, under his desk, in the toy chest. He looked out the window and saw nothing but the rain.

He ducked into his parents' room, and looked in everything that could have held Will, and everything that couldn't, not caring that they'd find out when they saw the mess he made.

The guest room was just as empty.

"Will?"

The bathroom echoed thunder.

"Will!"

He was sweating now, and he couldn't stop his fingers from snapping, couldn't stop his lips from moving as if he were talking to himself. He checked the hall closet, but it was locked. He shook the door as hard as he could, then turned the bolt over and reached in for the string that snapped on the light.

Something fell against his legs, and he jumped back, yelping, then scowling at an empty shoebox that had dropped from the high shelf.

When he turned the light on, he saw nothing, not even when he crammed himself in and pushed everything aside that he could move, or kick, or butt with his hips.

Will wasn't there.

He stood in the middle of the hall, turning in a tight circle and yanking his head away from the lightning.

"Will, where *are* you?"

In the bathroom, a faucet began dripping.

"*Will!*"

Downstairs, then, into the living room, the dining room, the coat closet, the pantry.

He raced through the den, and heard Bernadette still talking about corpses in old England.

He flung open the front door and stood in the rain, not caring how wet he was getting, just hoping to catch a glimpse of Stacey returning with fat Will in tow. He ran around the house and screamed over the storm into the shrubbery, into the garage, into the hedging that whipped at his arms and drew blood on his cheek.

"Stacey!" A cry more than a shout.

"Will!" Begging more than demanding.

There was no one in the toolshed, no one in the well.

He plunged back inside and stood by the table.

"Bernie."

She sighed, lightning flared, and the lamp flickered out.

"Bernie, answer me!"

He swung his arm and knocked over the bowl of popcorn. He kicked the table's near leg and toppled the glasses of soda. He picked up a chocolate bar and flung it at the hearth.

"Bernie, damnit!"

"Now that," she said, "is one of the things your father objects to. That kind of language."

"But—"

"And not paying attention. He said—they all said—none of you pays the slightest attention to them." She turned her head; he could see it moving though he couldn't see her eyes. "I could see that the first time I came here. And I could see something else, something rather sad, when you think about it a bit."

He shook his head and felt the water scattering across the room. "I don't give a damn about them now," he said, grabbing the card table by its edges and tipping it to the floor. "I want to know what you did with Will and Stacey!"

"You see, Jeremy, there are some people who just aren't cut out to be parents. They haven't the innate skills, or the temperament for it. Soon enough, they learn that children aren't pets, they're real human beings, and that's quite a revelation, don't you think? That children are human beings?"

He started to cry. He couldn't help it. Frustration at her refusal to respond made him so angry he couldn't stop the tears, or the way his legs stiffened as he kicked aside the wreckage and started to walk towards her.

"You, of course, didn't help very much," she said in light scolding.

"Bernie, please!"

"So your father found someone who knew me. And I came to help them get over their problem."

He stopped.

He could hear the soft whisper of Bernie's dress as she pushed out of the chair; he could hear the moist rattling of her breath in her throat; he could hear the odd way her feet struck the carpet as she walked over to meet him.

"Now, do you remember what I said about bog butter, Jeremy?"

He took a deep breath, closed his eyes, and screamed, "I don't care!"

"Ah, but you should, dear, you should."

There was lightning, and he gasped.

"They thought, you see, it was a curious little by-product of decomposition."

There was thunder, and the lamp flickered.

"It isn't, you know."

The lamp steadied, and he saw her, saw her soft silken dress and her soft silken hair and the glistening yellow wax that covered her soft silken arms.

"It's protection, my love."

He backed away, and screamed.

The lamp sizzled and went out.

"It keeps us alive. So we can help those who need us." She laughed then, and moved closer. "Now what are you afraid of, dear Jeremy my love. Why don't you tell me so I can show you what it's like."

ACKNOWLEDGMENTS

Special thanks to Kim Lim, Sara Broecker, Chad Buffington (Writers House LLC), Linda Smith, Chuck Verrill, Yessenia Santos (Simon & Schuster, Inc.), Violeta Mitrova (Hodder and Stoughton), David Drake, Kathryn Ptacek, Mandy Slater, and Jo Fletcher, for their help with compiling this volume.

ABOUT THE EDITOR

STEPHEN JONES lives in a neat house in London, England, surrounded by old books and movie posters. Since leaving school many, many years ago, he has done what he loves and loved what he does—writing and editing more than 150 scary books, and winning all sorts of awards for his work. His numerous volumes have included the illustrated histories *The Art of Horror* and *The Art of Horror Movies*, the tie-in books to the Neil Gaiman movies *Coraline* and *Stardust*, the critical studies *Horror: 100 Best Books* and *Horror: Another 100 Best Books* (both with Kim Newman), and *The Illustrated Monster Movie Guide*. Steve began reading comic books and monster movie magazines when he was a teenager and has never stopped.

ABOUT THE ARTIST

RANDY BROECKER was born in a decade when horror was king in comics—especially such EC titles as *Tales from the Crypt*. Thanks to his older brother, he developed a taste for horror and fantasy in books and movies as well. He has been crafting his superbly sickening illustrations and providing them to various putrid publications for over forty ghastly years. His art has graced the stories of such luminaries as Ray Bradbury, Ramsey Campbell, Neil Gaiman, and Tanith Lee, among many, many others. Although primarily associated with the horror genre (particularly all things Lovecraftian), he also wrote the book *Fantasy of the 20th Century*, a World Fantasy Award–nominated coffee-table art book he compiled for Collector's Press. He has also contributed art to record covers and video games. Randy lives in a very old house in Chicago, where he is content to draw monsters all day.